Bryn's Flight

ZODIAC ASSASSINS BOOK 8

ARTEMIS CROW

Bryn's Flight

Printed in the United States of America

First Printing, 2021

Print Book ISBN 978-1-7352644-9-3

Cover art by DAZED Design

OTHER BOOKS BY ARTEMIS CROW

Dedication

For the real Ashton, a horse who got his second chance at life and love, and for all the other beautiful souls—horse, dog, cat, and more—who deserve the same.

1

Bryn worked her way through the sweaty, testosterone-drenched cretins who'd tightly packed the center of the cavernous shipping warehouse that squatted in the mountains of Nowhere Colorado, somewhere between Aspen and Twin Lakes. She could scarce breathe in the thick cloud of body odor, beer, and blood without gagging. The crowd reeked of bloodlust, their feral energy barely contained. She certainly couldn't hear anything over the shouting. You'd think they were in a Roman coliseum the way the men were carrying on.

Not that her own horde was much better when they battled, but at least they were civilized, their violence studied, controlled. That was when they could fight; now they barely had the energy or will to survive.

If she failed here…

She had slipped past two men when one of them grabbed her ass and squeezed. What? To see if she was plump for the picking? That was another difference between these humans and the horde; pawing wasn't allowed.

She whipped her hand back and gripped the offending appendage, wrenching it around as she turned, the man's thumb bent back until it was close to breaking.

The man dropped to his knees and cried out.

"You don't touch, ever," she said.

He whimpered louder, his free hand clawing at her grip. She leaned close to the rude bastard.

"You aren't worth the effort," she said, ending her statement with a growl.

She planted a boot in his chest and shoved him away. She'd returned to her search when another hand grabbed her wrist and jerked her back.

"That's my brother you put hands on," said a larger, uglier version of the man on the floor.

"He needs to learn some manners. Maybe you ought to see to that before you let him out in public again," she said, jerking out of the man's grasp.

He lunged, and pulled her against him, her back to his belly. He wrapped his arms around her upper body, to immobilize her. "No one puts their hands on me or my family."

Bryn closed her eyes and smiled, the tension she'd carried for days easing. That was all she needed to hear.

"I couldn't agree more."

She dropped her head and rounded her shoulders as much as her attacker's arms would allow, then threw herself backward, slamming her head into his nose, breaking it if the sickening *crunch* told the tale.

The warm liquid splashing against the back of her neck? Gross. Although, since it was the blood of her adversary, that made it not so gross.

His soprano-worthy scream? Delightful.

He dropped her and reeled back, cupping his nose. The crowd around him parted until there was open floor. Bryn had wiped her hands together, job done, when asshole number one jumped up and roared. He crouched low and ran at her, his arms out in front, questing for a grab.

Bryn turned sideways to the man, bent her knees, and clenched her right fist. She waited until she could smell the halitosis jetting out of his mouth, then stepped forward with her left foot, and twisted her torso to the left. She backhanded the man before he could touch her.

Fist, meet temple.

8

He was unconscious before he hit the floor.

She stood tall and raised her head. "Uh-oh."

Every man in her immediate vicinity had stopped shouting; they'd even stopped drinking to focus their attention on her, their eyes growing beadier by the second.

She smiled and raised her hands. "All good, gents. Nothing to see here."

The throng didn't move, even when a bell rang and a roar echoed through the massive warehouse. Another fight over.

Time to go.

Bryn backed up a step and hit a wall of flesh. She whirled, ready to fight, but all she saw was a flat stomach covered in blue, black, and red tartan flannel. She tilted her head back to see a mountain of a man, noting the craggy face, a mop of dark brown hair, and beautiful, hazel eyes. Surprisingly handsome, and, wow, did he ever smell good.

She took a deep sniff. Yep, that was him alright. An oasis of woods and water and moss amid the unfettered stench.

The giant gently took her by the arm and turned her around. "Mr. C wants to see you."

She tried to peel back one of the thick, sausage fingers gripping her arm, but even she couldn't budge that kielbasa.

"They started it," she said, hating the petulant phrase that was unworthy of a warrior, even if it was the truth.

"Mr. C will finish it."

With that, Paul Bunyan—because all this mountain was missing was a blue ox—marched her to a hallway that led to a suite of offices. He passed all the regular-sized doors—he probably couldn't fit through them without great effort—in favor of the double doors at the very end.

Of course.

He opened both doors and pulled her inside.

The doors closed, not by magic, but by two hulking henchmen. They weren't the same size as Paul, but they were open carrying.

She didn't do guns.

Paul hauled her to the red, leather-covered desk festooned with ridiculously ornate, gold-leaf scrolls, and forced her to sit in a chair. Then he parked himself behind said chair and placed a platter-sized hand on top of her head, holding it there as if she were five years old and she couldn't leave the table until she ate her carrots.

She hated carrots.

Mr. C kicked back in his reclining throne and placed his fancy, red and black, silver-tipped Western boots on the desk. Add in jingle-jangle spurs and a Stetson hat and she could have broken out with a few *yeehaws* and not felt the least bit embarrassed.

He studied Bryn through the steam erupting like a geyser out of a large, cone-shaped machine.

No wonder the stink of the warehouse had vanished.

"What is that?" she asked with a sniff.

He flapped a dismissive hand once in the general direction of the steam. "A diffuser. Girlfriend thinks I need it to stay calm."

Bryn took a deeper sniff. "Frankincense, sandalwood, and…" She closed her eyes. "Lavender."

Mr. C nodded once. "Very good, but you're not here to sniff out the oils in my diffuser."

"And I imagine you need to stay calm considering you have a wife *and* a girl-friend," she said, glancing at the dirty, worn, gold band on his left ring finger.

His neutral expression dropped into a frown; the man didn't like to be called out.

Mr. C snapped his fingers and pointed at the security monitors occupying a good portion of the wall to her right. "You took down two men."

Paul obliged and turned her head to the screens.

She nodded when the first man grabbed her butt. "An asshole puts a hand on me, I put a hand on him. The idiot objected."

"That asshole and idiot are my sons."

Bryn sat very still and wondered at the vagaries of the universe. Not how she'd planned to introduce herself, but if her training had taught her anything, it was how to roll with the little upsets in life.

She fought against the hand holding her head so she could look Mr. C in the eye. "Seems they need a little training up before they're let loose in society again."

His eyes narrowed—so that's where his sons got their beady peepers—and pondered her for more than a long minute.

She was about to get antsy when he slapped the top of the desk and turned his focus on the giant. "You got any slots open tonight?"

She tried to turn her head to look up, but Paul squeezed her head a little tighter, keeping her in place.

"Slot? What do you mean by slot?" she asked, when she found her words.

"A fighting slot," Mr. C said.

"There's Jimmy. He's been wanting a fight."

Mr. C shook his head. "Nah, Jimmy'd never hit her, he's too soft on the ladies. Probably ask her to marry him," he added, "if it weren't for that road-kill-ugly scar on her face."

Bryn bit the inside of her cheek to keep from laughing at what the human thought to be an insult. Instead, she stuck her bottom lip out and gave him her best I've-been-whipped look.

"Aw, did I hurt your feelings?" Mr. C asked in a soft, chiding voice.

She stuck her lip out farther since she couldn't nod with Paul holding her head.

"Good."

That was the moment Bryn decided she didn't like Mr. C. She definitely didn't like his sons.

Mr. C dropped his feet, placed his elbows on the desk, and leaned forward. "Why are you here? This isn't a place women come to, except for the adventurous whores who don't mind the rough trade. The men out there get their juices up and they want to stick it hard to anything that can't run away."

Correction: She hated Mr. C.

"I came to fight."

"Oh, you're going to get a fight. The question is: Who can I put you in the ring with to teach you a lesson without killing you? I don't like dealing with dead bodies." He waved a hand in front of his face. "It's the smell."

"And the mess," Paul added.

Mr. C pointed at him and nodded. "Too right."

Correct the correction: She loathed Mr. C with the fury of the fire giant Surt fighting the god Freyr during Ragnarök.

"I already know who I want to fight," Bryn said to get them to shut up.

"Well, it couldn't be Buddy," Mr. C said. "He's even bigger than Ira here."

She jerked her head hard to free it because she *had* to see the giant's face. But no go. "Your name is Ira? Your parents named you that when you're this big?"

"I wasn't born this big." Ira grunted and pressed down a little on her head like he was trying to compress her spine. "Family name."

"They named him after his mom's favorite Chi-Weenie dog. The little, bitey bastard," Mr. C added helpfully.

Bryn could feel Ira tremble through the grip he had on her head. Scratch helpfully—the gleam in Mr. C's eyes spoke of cruelty, not an interest in "the more you know." He was the type to belittle and bully until you were down, then crush you out of existence.

Bryn savaged the inside of her cheek this time because she had to survive this interview. Too much was riding on getting into the ring with the right person. Neither laughter nor derision would get her what she wanted.

"It's not Buddy, whoever he is," she said. "And what's with all the names ending in Y? Jimmy, Buddy? I mean, come on."

"We're simple folk here in Colorado," Mr. C said, his frown pulling his jowls down. "You'd know that if you were from these parts. You'd also know that no one messes with my kin."

She held up her hands. "Alright, fine. I'm sorry I hurt your precious boys. Are we good?"

"You aren't getting away from the pile of shit you stepped in that easily, girlie." He sat back, laced his fingers, and rested them over his belly. "Tell me, who'd you come to fight?"

She folded her hands in her lap and smiled sweetly, ignoring the stretch of the scar on the left side of her face, pleased when Mr. C flinched in disgust. Her scar had been hard won and she was proud of it. Didn't mean she couldn't have fun grossing out any human in her vicinity, though.

"I came here to fight your undefeated champion. I came here to fight Rota."

Mr. C and Ira remained completely still. So still Bryn itched to snap her fingers to wake them up from the hypnotic trance she'd inadvertently put them in.

But she needn't have worried.

All four men in the room burst out laughing at the same time, as if they had coordinated the move for the greatest, most insulting effect.

Correct the corrected correction: She wanted to flay the men with flames from the god of fire Loki himself, until all that remained of them was ash.

2

It took the men far too long to stop their tear-inducing guffaws. Bryn sat in sullen silence until they finally wound down.

Mr. C pulled a handkerchief out of his back pocket and dabbed at his face to dry it before lobbing a box of tissues like a football at the two men guarding the door.

Ira decided to forego a tissue, using his sleeve to swipe at his tears and the snotty nose that she couldn't see, but could hear because he sniffled every five seconds.

"You want to get in the ring with Rota?" Mr. C asked, a fresh round of laughter bursting out of him. "She'll eat you alive and spit out your bones."

Bryn's spine snapped straight at the insult the human couldn't possibly realize he'd made. "I took care of your sons well enough."

Mr. C's laughter stopped abruptly. "You'd be smart to keep your mouth shut and your hands to yourself where they're concerned. Do I have to warn you a second time?"

Yep, that got his attention.

"No, I got it," she said, in a sing-song voice.

His eyes narrowed again.

"I came to fight Rota. If she's so good that she can wipe the floor with me, why not put me in the ring with her to teach me a lesson?"

"She's got a point," Ira said.

Ever the helper, that one.

"Teddy is slated to fight her tonight," Mr. C said.

Bryn bit the inside of her already abused cheek to stop the snark poised on her tongue. Another name ending in Y. Seriously? Any moment now, her mouth was going to start bleeding from all the biting.

She managed to remain silent, though, waiting for the men to work it out.

"Teddy will do whatever you tell him," Ira pointed out.

"That he will, that he will." The boss man studied her for a moment, before picking up his phone. "Sully."

Bryn closed her eyes and held her breath. *Do not laugh, do not laugh.*

"Tell Teddy he's off the slate tonight. He'll get his chance next week. Yeah, I know he'll be mad, but tell him I said so. If he doesn't like it, he can go fight for some other outfit."

He listened for a bit.

"I have another fighter for Rota." He looked at Bryn and sneered. "It's going to be a bloodbath, so tell her to wear her old costume so she can just throw the bloody rags away."

Bryn smiled broadly.

"Just so," she said under her breath.

He hung up the phone and linked his fingers together. "Take her to the locker room, the far one."

"That one's still being repaired," Ira said. "No one's supposed to go in there."

"You will with her. Make sure she doesn't run."

Mr. C waved a hand in the direction of the door. Ira winced; Bryn could feel the movement through his hand on her head.

"I mean it, Ira, don't take your eyes off her for a minute. Now go. I want her ready in time."

Ira squeezed Bryn's head and lifted her straight out of the chair.

Not fun, but at least her spine straightened to its normal length with a *pop-pop-pop*. The huge man turned her toward the doors before releasing her head and taking her arm.

Bryn looked back at Mr. C's gloating expression. "With a wife and a girlfriend, you might need to keep your energy up. Try adding some urushiol oil to the diffuser. It'll give you an experience you'll never forget."

Ira pulled her through the doors, which closed behind the pair.

"Come on. You're getting what you want," he said, leading her down the hallway. "You're not going to like it."

Bryn trotted to keep up with the man. There was no staying next this guy without some hustle up.

They entered the main warehouse again in time for the crowd to roar their pleasure, their fists jabbing and uppercutting the air as if they were the combatants slugging it out. Ira turned right and they walked next to the outer wall down half the length of the warehouse until they reached a large swinging door.

Ira pushed it open and turned sideways to enter, Bryn squished hard against his flat, rock-hard gut. Again. Damn, that smell seemed to be his own, not cologne or detergent. She took a deep breath of the intoxicating scent; her thighs quivered in response.

They popped through and she exhaled as they separated, regretting that she couldn't pull him closer and fill her lungs again.

"Whoa," she called out when he jerked her forward, almost pulling her off her feet in his rush.

They walked down a hall, passing a locker room filled with half-naked and completely naked men—stellar specimens they were not. Despite Ira's best efforts to shield her from the view, she saw more than she wanted to remember.

"Sure is cold here in Colorado," she remarked, trying to blink it all away.

"Not this time of year," Ira said, completely missing the point.

She rolled her eyes and looked ahead. There was a door to their right with a women's restroom sign on it that someone had Picassoed with ginormous, lopsided boobs in Sharpie.

"The Louvre is calling," she whispered under her breath as they passed it by for the plastic-tarp-blocked doorway at the end.

Bryn reached out and ran the tips of her fingers along the drywall separating the hallway from the main part of the warehouse. The wall vibrated under the onslaught of the crowd's clomping and clapping and cheering, the veneer of the wall as thin as the veneer of civility on the other side.

Like the thin veneer between the four worlds that had been pierced recently after holding for centuries.

Like the thin veneer between the species, between protection and persecution, between life and death.

Like the thin veneer between hope and despair that had ripped open for the horde, leaving broken shards of loss and pain. Shards that had cut her until she walked away from everything she valued to come here on what she hoped wasn't a fool's errand.

Yet the deepest, darkest part of her heart feared she was the fool.

Ira pulled the tarp aside, breaking her introspection; it wasn't productive. She rolled her shoulders back and blew out a breath. Time to tuck her fears away. If you wanted something too much, you rarely got it.

He walked her to the sole bank of four lockers and opened the one that had "Rota" scrawled on it, again in Sharpie. Inside lay a folded pile of clothes.

"There are shorts and a sports bra for you. And a chest protector. Boss doesn't want any women's parts to get hurt, you know, for when you have babies."

Ira's blush started before he even finished the sentence.

Bryn snorted at the thought. *Babies. As if.*

Even if she had wanted children, the horde had not only stopped fighting, they'd also stopped nearly everything else, including conceiving. The only reason for coming here, for subjecting herself to the presence of humans, for disobeying an express command not to ask Rota the betrayer for a damn thing, was to save their lives.

She pulled out the skimpy and stretched-out, black-and-gold shorts and sports bra and put them on a wobbly bench. "Ira, you're going to have to release my arm so I can get dressed."

He pursed his lips but let her go. The man seemed a lot nicer than his boss.

Wonder how he ended up here?

She raised a forefinger and gave it a whirl. "Turn around."

"Mr. C said I had to keep my eyes on you at all times," he said, his discomfort obvious.

"Okay. Guess I'll do the turning."

She turned away from him and pulled her shirt out of her jeans, unbuttoning it quickly. She dropped the shirt on the bench then removed her bra.

Ira sucked in a breath. "Oh, that must have hurt."

She knew the visage her back presented; the brand and the scars from training and fighting. The horses she'd tried to fly and couldn't. Years of injury and damage had riddled her with the evidence of her failures, yet she didn't care about the appearance of the scars; she cared that they existed at all.

Tonight would change everything.

Bryn dropped her pants, standing naked in front of the man guarding her. Again, Ira hissed at the sight of the deep, jagged scars, but this time he didn't comment. There was nothing to be said, by either of them.

She slipped on the shorts, the chest protector, and the sports bra, then faced Ira.

"Like to keep your women fighters scantily clad, don't you?" she said, tugging the very skimpy, very tight shorts out of places the material wasn't meant to be.

His face was beet red. He hadn't looked away, not for a second, and he was abashed by the experience.

Sweet.

"The men only wear a cup and shorts."

Bryn stepped into the huge guy, stood on her toes, but still fell far short of his impressive height. She pounded his shoulder with the flat of her hand; her manner gruff to reassure him. "It's okay, Ira."

Strange that she could feel sorry for the man.

She pulled her silver and black-striped hair back and took an elastic band from an open bag in the locker. Securing the thick mass, she rolled her neck. "I'm ready. Is it time?"

A bell rang and the crowd roared. The bout had ended.

He nodded. "Come."

Ira led her quickly past the men's locker room—this time she studied the floor to avoid the vista of flesh, such as it was—and into the open space of the warehouse.

The packed crowd stepped aside to give Ira room to pass, the spectators' gazes falling on Bryn and staying there, their speculation almost as sure as a touch. She wouldn't have been surprised to have them reach out and squeeze her biceps and quads, or pat her rippled abs or her developed deltoids to check the thick muscle she'd curated over the years. Hell, with this crowd she wouldn't have been surprised if they'd checked her teeth, like horse traders.

Bryn didn't care, though; she only had eyes for the chain-link cage.

Before they reached it, Mr. C and his henchmen pushed their way through the crowd and stopped them.

"Hold here a second while I announce the fight," Mr. C said, one arm on Ira, the opposite hand holding a microphone.

Ira nodded once and held Bryn back, surrounded by spectators so thick that she couldn't see inside the cage fully, just the top half.

The microphone squawked; her heart flopped in her chest. She closed her eyes and breathed slow and deep as she listened to the blowhard announce that there had been a change in fighters for the premiere bout of the night.

The crowd muttered and shifted restlessly.

Mr. C went through what seemed like an old sales spiel about his business and cage fighting and buying a premium membership, going on and on until Bryn's calm started to fray. Finally, he announced Rota. No fanfare, no windup; he just said the name and the men went wild. Even Ira's grip on her arm tightened.

The chain-link gate squeaked as it opened.

The chant "Rota, Rota, Rota," started to Bryn's left and wound its way through the crowd until the din was deafening. Just when she thought they would never shut up, Mr. C announced that a new fighter had come to challenge Rota.

"That's our cue," Ira said, pulling her forward.

They reached the entrance and the crowd murmured when they saw her, talking among themselves as they assessed her.

Ira pulled her inside the ring and released her arm. But Bryn barely felt her freedom; her eyes were on Rota's back as the woman gripped the cage fence and leaned into it, her head down.

Years.

It had taken Bryn years to get to this moment, years spent dreaming of learning under the greatest horsemaster the horde had ever known, years spent regretting that Rota had left the horde, never to return, years spent feeling her hero worship leach away until all she felt for Rota was bile's bitter taste.

Years spent watching the horde slowly fade away.

But the years of searching for Rota in the human world were over; creating the opportunity to help her people was finally here. She could not fail.

"Hey, what's your name?" Mr. C asked, leaning close with his hand over the open mic. "So I can introduce you, and for your tombstone."

He laughed, his bodyguards joining in after a beat.

Sycophants.

Bryn kept her eyes on Rota's back, anticipation about to choke her. "Just call me…Valkyrie."

3

"Gentlemen!" Mr. C yelled into the microphone. "This is going to be a bloody one, so put on your raincoats or tarps if you've got 'em! With us tonight, straight from I-Don't-Know-Where-And-I-Don't-Care, US of A…" He paused while the crowd roared. "I give you…Valkyrie!"

Bryn's ears rang from the noise, but her focus remained on her opponent.

Rota oh so slowly raised her head, still looking forward.

Bryn smiled. Oh, yeah, she'd heard the name. She knew what it meant.

Rota dropped her hands and turned around to face Bryn, her face devoid of any emotion, her stance relaxed and ready for what Bryn might bring, but her dark eyes had a fire in them. "Staring into a flame" it was called; it spoke of battles fought and won, of choosing who lived and died, of carrying the slain to Valhalla to wait by Odin's side for the start of Ragnarök. It spoke of the blood that had soaked their kind for centuries.

Rota might have left the Valkyrie, but she hadn't forgotten who and what she was.

Bryn took a step forward and Rota matched it, both women assessing.

Rota was taller than Bryn, and her body broader, with the depth and thickness of muscle that only years of training could build. She hadn't lost any of her strength—fighting men and winning proved that—and it didn't appear that she'd lost any of her renowned courage. But what about her will to fight? Had she softened over the years? Had she reduced her training to just what she needed to win against humans?

Humans? Really? The warrior had obviously fallen far, and Bryn would use that against her to win this fight and make Rota return to the horde and help her people.

Bryn finally looked hard at the woman's face.

Dark brown skin stretched over high cheekbones with crosshatched scars. Another scar cut through the middle of her right eyebrow, bisecting the arched peak. Her jaw was square and strong, her lips were full and soft, a contrast to the hard planes of her face. The dark eyes with a hint of blue spoke of a knowing that only came with the passage of time and the pain that too often accompanied it.

The woman was beautiful, fierce…and tired, old in Valkyrie years.

Rota walked closer then circled Bryn. "Valkyrie? Really? A bit on the nose, isn't it?"

Bryn watched her, her body tensed for attack. "Like these humans would ever get it."

"That's no reason to get sloppy. And you are sloppy, based on the ruckus you caused earlier."

Bryn walked around Rota; two could play this game. "Saw that, did you?"

"No, heard it. And you got Mr. C's attention. Not smart."

Bryn spread her arms. "What do you call what you're doing?"

"My business."

The crowd jeered, restlessness for a fight turning ugly fast.

"Well, I'm making you my business now." Bryn stopped stalking and waved Rota to her. "Let's get on with it."

"If you win," Rota said, "what do you want?"

Bryn had to press her lips firmly together to keep from smiling. The woman was already conceding. "When I win, you'll return to the Valkyrie."

Rota snorted. "When I win, you'll leave and never bother me again."

Bryn crouched, her hands up. "Agreed. Let's do this."

Rota remained loose, her hands by her sides, her knees straight. She stopped moving and just stood there, her feet shoulder-width apart.

Bryn lunged, closing the distance between them. She swept her arm around for a right hook that would knock Rota off her feet and out, unconscious. Down and out in one, that's how she rolled.

Her fist raced to Rota's cheek. It was just a whisper away from connecting when Rota turned her head ever so slightly away. Just enough that Bryn's fist missed, and she was thrown off balance.

Rota grabbed Bryn's ponytail, stopping the turn. She raised Bryn's head and kneed her in the solar plexus, before letting her go.

"Reckless."

Bryn bent over and staggered back as she gagged, choking on the pain, fighting to get air into her lungs. The men outside the cage yelled and jerked on the chain-link, rattling it hard.

Rota backed away and crossed her arms over her chest. "You done?"

Bryn finally pulled in a deep breath, the air clearing her head. She stood as tall as her quivering gut allowed and shook her head. "I'm just getting started."

Rota strode up to Bryn and shoved her before punching her in the face with a right cross.

Bryn turned with the punch to mitigate the damage, then ducked under Rota's left and did a one-two punch to Rota's midsection, sending Rota back.

They squared off, fists raised. The warmup was done; time to get serious.

Back and forth they moved, punching, kicking, matching each other blow for blow. The crowd roared for every landed punch and kick, the noise battering.

Bryn panted as the spreading pain fought for her attention, but Rota didn't seem to be affected. Rota had some blood on her face too—thank the Allfather—but not nearly enough, and the woman had barely broken a sweat. She merely seemed annoyed; she certainly hadn't slowed a bit.

Damn her to Hel's wrath.

Bryn had lifted a foot to back away and give herself a moment to catch her breath when Rota's fist connected with her left eye.

Little, white lights twinkled; the sting of blood and sweat caused her to tear up, which set her nose to running. *Lovely...*

Bryn shook her head to clear it, then lunged forward—well, more like fell—the move getting under Rota's defenses. Bryn grabbed Rota's arms and kneed her in the gut three times.

Rota grunted and went down on one knee.

Bryn staggered back a couple steps, her head woozy from the effort, her feet spread wide, arms dangling. "You will come back with me. You will save the Valkyrie and live the life you were destined for. Quit now and come with me, before you embarrass yourself."

She swayed for a moment before she caught herself. Rota dropped her head and raised a hand, her ribs heaving.

"You're done," Bryn said, gloating.

She'd thought it would be nearly impossible to get Rota back to the horde. All this time worrying for nothing.

The crowd slowly grew silent.

Bryn turned to face them and raised her arms. "I am your new—"

A freight train hit her in the back. That could be the only explanation for the force that threw Bryn forward and slammed her down on the floor. That same train sat on her butt and reached down. A thick arm Bryn couldn't imagine a train having wrapped around her neck and pulled.

Bryn's back bowed until she had to plant her hands on the floor to give her spine a break, before it did break.

She gagged, kicking her lower legs the best she could, but Rota was like a freaking bear: huge, heavy, and pissed.

The lights in the warehouse dimmed.

Ah, mood lighting for the killing. How nice.

Rota pressed the side her face against Bryn's head to whisper in her ear. "You shouldn't have come here, pup. Go home and don't let me see you again, or I *will* kill you."

Rota grabbed Bryn's ponytail again and slammed her forehead once, twice, three times against the concrete floor.

Once would have been enough to convince Bryn that she'd lost. Twice seemed to be because Rota wanted to make sure. Three times, well, that was just showing off.

Bryn sagged into Rota's hold and let Fate decide what to do with her, because she'd had all her fucks beaten out of her, leaving her a mess like when she was a toddler with her first wooden sword, a dirty diaper, and drool running down her chin.

Embarrassing didn't even begin to cover it. But who really cared about their pride when there were all those pretty, pretty lights floating around?

The bear decided it had had enough and the great weight was lifted off Bryn. She lay on the cool concrete, grateful for the comfort, more grateful to be horizontal, less grateful that she'd have to return empty-handed to the endless funeral pyres and the hollow eyes of the haggard horde.

Cheers pummeled her, the rude bastards, and Mr. C announced that Rota was the undefeated champion.

Ira's boat-sized boots made an appearance by her face. "Time to go, Valkyrie."

"Yeah, yeah," she muttered.

He gently rolled her onto her back then picked her up and carried her out of the ring.

4

Several mortifying minutes later—for her and for Ira—he had changed her into her clothes. He was so red she was afraid for his health. She, however, was horrified by the humiliation Rota had so handily dealt her.

Ira bent to pick her up again, but she held up a hand to stop him. He backed away.

"I'm good to walk," she said, trying to keep her tone soft as she struggled to sit up then stand.

The big guy was trying to help; Ira didn't deserve her ira. She fought against the giggle that percolated around her chest.

Ira doesn't deserve my ira. Heh.

"Mr. C said you have to go, and don't come back."

She wanted to snort, it was her go-to reaction after all, but her face hurt too much, and she was afraid her nose would gush blood if she forced air through it too fast. "I figured."

"I'll walk you to the door," he said, holding the tarp aside for her.

She kept her eyes forward and one hand on the wall to help her balance. A hot flush filled her. Not from embarrassment this time, but from her body telling her it had had enough. She needed to sleep and recuperate so she could plan what to do next to get Rota to return to the horde. She might have been trounced in the cage, but she couldn't go back empty-handed. There had to be a way to convince Rota that the Valkyrie needed her more than Rota needed her freedom.

Ira opened the exit door and held it for Bryn, then fell in beside her as she entered the parking lot.

"I'm good, Ira."

"My mom taught me to always walk a lady to her car."

"Lady? I don't think I've ever been called that before."

"Why? That's what you are."

They reached her car and she turned to the giant of a man. She pressed a palm to his chest, right over his heart, ignoring the hot, sharp ache in her swollen, split-skin knuckles. "Why are you working here? You are too nice for this place."

"I have to make money."

"But you could be a bouncer at a club, make better money, maybe even tips."

He shook his head, his floppy brown hair falling forward. "I scare the customers too much, especially the ladies."

The wistful expression on his face was sad to see.

"Well, they're fools, Ira. You're a good man, and coming from me, that's saying a lot."

She dropped her hand and turned to unlock her car door.

"Uh, Valkyrie?"

"Yes?"

"What's your real name?"

She smiled then grimaced when her bottom lip broke open again and blood oozed down her chin. She wiped it away with a finger and flicked the blood onto the asphalt. "My name is Bryn."

Ira smiled, showing a mouthful of beautiful teeth, and turning him a downright *aw shucks* kind of handsome. "Night, Bryn."

"Good night, Ira," she called out as he walked away. "And goodbye," she whispered.

She opened her car door and climbed inside, groaning when she sat, every muscle complaining about the mistreatment.

She rested her arms on the steering wheel, tempted to close her eyes and sleep right here rather than drive to the motel, but the thought of a lukewarm shower and a soft, albeit lumpy, bed was too great a siren call.

She had reached for the keys to start the engine when the door to the warehouse opened, and a young blonde woman was walked out by one of Mr. Cs goons. Well, more like dragged out since she was clawing and kicking the man.

"Barbie at the fights. Will wonders never cease?"

The goon half threw the girl forward. He said something while shaking a finger at her. She, feisty little minx that she was proving to be, spat at him and stamped a foot.

"That'll never work, girlie," Bryn said with a chuckle.

She started the engine and turned the heated seat to high, waiting for the engine to warm enough so she could turn on the heater. The former would start loosening up her muscles; the latter would take the edge off the cold Colorado mountain night.

She watched the show until the goon went back inside the warehouse and Barbie stormed off into the parking lot. Seemed Ira was the only gentleman in the place.

The seat warmed her bum and warm air finally flowed over her skin. *Time to go.*

She pulled forward and took a right, idling slowly down the row of cars to the first opening that would take her to the exit. *Gotta go slow with the number of people drinking inside.* Taking out a human with her car was a mess she didn't have the time nor the inclination to deal with, so caution ruled the day…or night, as it were.

She had almost reached an opening in the row when she heard the bellow of a very angry female.

She braked and listened. Yep, there it was again. Somebody was hollering for all she was worth, and Bryn had to wonder if it was Barbie. The girl might have been feisty, but she was slim and very young, not a person Bryn would want to watch her back in a fight.

Barbie alone? Not good.

Bryn put the car in park and opened the door, stepping out to look around. A scuffle sounded in front and to the left of her.

She eased the door closed and pocketed her keys before walking quietly in the direction of what was definitely a scuffle, supporting her weight with a hand on each car she passed. Rounding a line of trucks, she found Asshole and Idiot and two other men in a circle around Barbie, shoving her from one man to the other, pawing at her when they had their turn.

Barbie was spitting mad, like cat-getting-a-bath mad, but the gleam in the men's eyes made Bryn twitch. That gleam could shift to intent at any moment and Barbie's anger would morph into a terror that would haunt the girl forever.

Bryn wasn't in any shape to take on four men after Rota's beat down, but she couldn't stand aside and let Barbie get hurt and carry that wound for the rest of her life. She took as deep a breath as she could.

"Ahem," Bryn said loudly. "I think her dance card is already full."

The man she'd come to think of as Asshole looked up. His remarkably small eyes nearly disappeared when he squinted at her, but—shazam—they became positively huge with recognition when he saw past her swollen face.

"Well, well, look who it is. The Valkyrie."

The other men stopped toying with Barbie and turned in unison to stare at her.

"That's the bitch who nearly broke my wrist," Idiot said.

One of the other men tilted his head and ran his gaze over her. "Looks like she's been tenderized for us. Y'all hungry as I am?"

"Starved," Asshole and Idiot said.

The four rushed Bryn.

She got in one great upper cut, knocking Asshole back, but her hand wasn't having it. White-hot pain shot up her arm and slammed into her chest, followed by a worrisome numbness.

Idiot punched her in the stomach, but she grabbed his shoulders to keep from going down, then hit him in the gut with her knee while pulling him forward. He hunched over and she used his body for balance to mule-kick one man in the knee, shoving the joint backward with a satisfying crunch.

He, however, was less satisfied and more screamy. He flopped onto the ground, clutching his broken knee. One down, three to go.

She shoved Idiot away just as Asshole reached her. She tried to pivot away from his wild swing, but Rota had wrought some powerful bad mojo on her body, and it said, "Uh, no, we're not moving that fast right now."

So what she had attempted to do to avoid the man's swing failed, and she paid the price. His hammer-sized fist hit her on the cheek, throwing her head to the side. Her neck cracked and she spun away, unable to stop the momentum that drove her into the ground.

Asshole, being the asshole that he was, didn't wait for her to get up like you would in a fair fight. Nope, he ran to her and sat on her hips, securing her flailing hands. "Now you're gonna find out why you don't mess with me or mine."

He lifted his arm and his fist walloped her. Her head flew to one side then rolled back until she could see the stars in the night sky. His other fist punched her, sending her head to the other side. Once again, she saw stars. Only this time they were doubled.

Over and over, he hit her until she lost count.

Then lost consciousness.

5

Something buzzed at her, while something else tugged on her arm. Bryn tried to open her eyes but they protested so much she gave up trying. A voice broke through the fog enough to rouse her.

"Come on, wake up, before they decide to come back," a girl shouted in her ear. Was the voice slapping her? It felt like it was slapping her.

A light burned one of her eyes.

Had she opened it? No, someone was prying her eyelid open and blinding her with the light of a thousand suns.

"Stop that," she managed to get out, not knowing if whoever was pestering her could understand the gibberish coming out from between her numb lips.

Then she started flying. Or rather, she was levitating. Levitating and floating around because a light passed by then it got dark again. Rinse and repeat.

"Get her in the back," the girl said.

A grunt rumbled against her aching ribs. She stopped floating and rested on a comfy surface, the air around her warm instead of chilly.

"Move over, I'm driving," a deep, male voice said.

"I have a learner's permit."

"No," the man said.

A door closed and an engine started.

The scent of woods and water and moss caressed her, and she relaxed.

The car lurched once, twice, then the movement smoothed out. The darkness all around her closed in tight, cocooning her, and she welcomed the relief.

* * *

Bryn opened her eyes and instantly wished she hadn't. Her aches and pains had aches and pains, which, combined, meant she was in agony. She tried to rise onto her elbows, but oh no, that wasn't happening anytime soon.

She blinked several times to focus, since rubbing her eyes was beyond her, then took in the room. It was huge, wider than most bedrooms she'd seen and very long. The floor was concrete and had large rugs covering most of it, except at the opposite end to her right. There, the floor had a group of rectangular, black mats sunk into it—a type Bryn hadn't seen before—that took up as much space as a twenty-by-twenty broodmare stall.

Yeah, the room was that big.

Spare, spartan, positively monastic, the room had four walls, of course, and two barn-stall-type sliding doors, one a closet, she assumed, while the other was an exit. She was occupying the largest piece of furniture, a dark, gothic, king-sized bed. Over the top for such a spare room, but having a gothic sensibility, she rather loved it. In addition, there was a matching dresser and armoire, and a chair and desk. Her clothes were draped over the lone chair, her duffle bag on the floor next to the desk, unopened.

She slowly rolled her head to the left. Light danced through the sheer, white curtains, the blue sky horrifyingly cheerful. Mother Nature had no business being that happy when she had been felled so low. Her state demanded thick, dark storm clouds and rain and thunder.

There were no photographs of smiling parents and giddy children, nothing to distinguish this room from any motel room she'd been in, save for the size, the fancy furniture, and the lack of the mysterious crustiness one usually found on the top blanket. She had refused to contemplate what said crustiness was, but she could guess that it wasn't sizing.

Voices drifted under the door: two women, one very excitable.

She heaved a sigh then groaned at the pain. There was nothing for it; she had to get up, get dressed and eat something to regain her strength.

She tried to sit up, but her belly said nope. She eased onto her side and pushed off the covers, exposing the fact that she was naked. Oh, joy, more strangers who'd gotten to ogle her while she was nude; only this time she'd been unconscious. Not that she cared about being bare-ass in front of people, but she preferred having a say about who saw her all-under and when.

Dropping her lower legs over the side, she used her arms to lever herself up, trying to keep her body in a straight line. She managed to rise to a sit, but she started panting and thought she'd heave if she moved again too soon. Bloody beatings took the stuffing out of you.

She'd had her share, but not two in less than an hour. Bryn took another deep breath and forced herself to stand, conceding that she needed to support herself with a hand on the headboard. If she went down now, she'd be on the floor for some time, and that would prove to be messy…and mortifying.

Stars danced a tango in front of her, her head spinning around trying to match their steps, but she clung to the headboard, her fingers laced with the many scrolls of the wood, staying upright until the dance ended. She took a step toward the chair and her clothes.

Okay, that wasn't so bad.

She let go of the headboard and took two more steps. Not great, but doable. Then the stars came out again. She wobbled her way to the chair and collapsed in it, her body shaking, sweat breaking out all over.

"This is ridiculous," she said, chiding her traitorous body.

But it had nothing more to say, not that it wasn't speaking loudly enough already.

Birds chirped, the wind blew, the world kept spinning around, and she was stuck. In more ways than one.

The door to the bedroom opened and Barbie bounced in, her step flying almost as high as her ponytail. But it was her blinding smile that almost had Bryn sliding out of the chair and crawling back to the bed.

Odin, please rid me of damn cheerful morning people.

"You're awake!" the girl chirped.

Bryn dropped her head into her hands. "And I'm naked."

"Oh, I won't hold that against you. I've already seen all of you from head to toe."

Bryn looked up and threw the girl her most withering glare, the one that sent shivers down the spines of the most ruthless scallywags in the Valkyrie ranks, but Miss Chirps-A-Lot smiled brighter, as if either immune or somehow knowing that the likelihood of Bryn thrashing the chirpy chippie was nonexistent.

Either way, Bryn needed to get the girl to leave, or she needed strong pain meds. Both would be preferable.

"Coffee?" Barbie said, bouncing on her toes.

"Oh, goddess, yes," Bryn groaned.

And just like that, Barbie left the room.

"Huh."

Bryn pulled the sweatpants she was sitting on out from under her butt and slowly put one foot through then the other, rocking side to side to get them over her hips. One down.

She slipped the tee shirt over her head and pulled it down just as Barbie trotted in, a blessedly huge coffee mug in one hand, staring at the edge to make sure she didn't spill.

She set it on the desk in front of Bryn and pulled out a wad of creamer and sugar packets, dumping them on the desk too. "I didn't know what you wanted, so I brought some of both."

"Black with a shitload of sugar is how I roll."

Bryn picked up all the sugar packets and organized them. Then she ripped the tops off the entire pile and dumped her greatest weakness into her mug.

"Wow, my mom would flay me alive if I had that much sugar at one time."

"Well, she's not here and she's not my mother."

Bryn stirred the hot liquid with a finger, barely wincing from the heat, then licked the coffee off it. She gripped the mug with both hands and proceeded to worship the bean god, whoever the hell he was.

The miracle drug, caffeine, started working immediately, or maybe it was just the fact that she wasn't lying dead on the side of the road that perked her up. Survival had that effect on her.

"What happened last night? And why isn't your mom here, eyeballing me for the stranger that I am?"

Barbie took a seat on the bed and started bouncing again.

Did I ever have that much energy at that age?

"After you got righteously walloped and passed out, Mr. C's sons and their friends got bored and left you. I ran inside and found Ira and he helped me get you in the car and he drove us here."

"And I got in here?"

"Ira carried you in and helped me undress you."

"Did he blush bright red?"

"Oh, I thought he was going to combust," Barbie said, giggling.

"Did he take my car?"

"Oh, no. He drove us back to the warehouse, and I drove your car here."

"Do you even have a license?"

Not that Bryn cared about human laws, but it seemed like the right thing to ask, being the adult in the room.

Barbie smiled so wide Bryn needed sunglasses. "Just a learner's permit. Isn't it great?"

"Did my car survive?"

Barbie gave her a peppy salute. "Yes, ma'am. Not a scratch or dent."

Bryn took another rejuvenating sip and held up a hand to stop her. "Easy, kid, you're gonna poke out my eyes with your enthusiasm." She glanced around the room again. "Is this yours?"

"Oh, no, it's Ashton's."

"Well, your brother has absolutely no artistic taste. I would have expected a poster of some half-naked woman, or some action movie stars, you know, stuff boys like."

Barbie cocked her head, her eyes twinkling. "Ashton isn't into that kind of stuff."

"I'll say," Bryn muttered, sipping her coffee.

"Because Ashton—"

"Helena!" a loud, female voice shouted through the house, interrupting the girl.

Ah, so Barbie was Helena. Much better name, though not as apt.

"Where are you?" the voice asked from much closer.

"Mother?" Bryn asked the girl.

Her eyes widened. "Uh."

Bryn decided standing was the best way to present herself. Odin knew, the rest of her wasn't presentable even without a mirror to tell her the full tale. She struggled to her feet, keeping one hand on the back of the chair, and waited as footsteps approached.

A strapping shadow breached the room first, followed by the strapping woman the shadow had presaged.

Bryn started laughing and collapsed into the chair.

Rota scowled, every impressive tooth in her mouth showing as she turned to Helena. "What the ever-living fuck is she doing in my house?"

6

"Rota is your mother?" Bryn asked after she caught her breath.

Helena shook her head. "What? No! She's my riding instructor."

"Not if you don't explain this," Rota spat, pointing at Bryn.

Helena's smile faltered. "I found her injured. You wouldn't want me to leave a woman bleeding, would you?"

Rota crossed her most impressive arms and scowled harder at the girl. "Not nearly good enough."

"It's true," Bryn added. "But not the whole story."

Rota raised a hand to stop Bryn from continuing. "Where did you find her, Helena?"

What remained of Helena's smile fell.

"At the fight," she whispered.

Rota stood so still Bryn was concerned the woman had stroked out on the spot. Until she saw the wave of flush start at Rota's hairline and crash down her face.

Even Bryn winced a little, a bead of sweat rolling down her spine. Oh, yeah, the woman was livid.

"You went to the fight?"

Helena raised her head and then her chin. She'd found a spark of courage and stoked it with defiance. "Yes."

"After I've told you for years that you cannot," Rota said, her voice ominously quiet, her hands curling into fists.

Helena dropped her head and stared at her feet; her shoulders rounded. Defiance defeated.

Bryn braced herself in case the woman decided to get corporal with her punishment. Bryn was many unpleasant things, and she was okay with that, but a bully wasn't one of them, nor was she abusive. Especially when Helena had already been through a scare. She slid her feet under her and spread them to get ready to lunge.

But Rota didn't raise her hands in anger. Instead, she stepped close to Helena, gently cupped the girl's face, and tipped it back.

She stared into Helena's eyes for a long moment. "Something happened."

Helena didn't obfuscate. "Yes."

"Tell me," Rota said softly but firmly, as if knowing the girl would cry if given too much sympathy.

"Caldwell's boys…"

"Did they hurt you?"

"No, but they were going to until she stepped in."

"Bryn, my name is Bryn."

Helena didn't look away from Rota. "Bryn stepped in so I could get away, and she took a bad beating."

"Well, some of this damage," Bryn added, pointing to her face, "was from Rota, but yeah."

Rota raised a hand, palm facing Bryn to shut her up.

"Helena?" Rota said in a whisper.

"Yes?"

"Are you okay?"

The sunshine that seemed to permeate every inch of the girl was suddenly snuffed out by clouds. Helena shook her head once then folded in on herself.

Rota said nothing. She simply wrapped her arms around Helena and held her tight.

Bryn sat perfectly still watching the pair, shocked by the compassion the famed—or infamous, depending on who you talked to—Rota had shown the girl.

It was beautiful.

Bryn shifted in her chair, discomfited by the obvious affection between the two, yet buoyed by the discovery of a weakness she could exploit in furtherance of her goal. A goal that suddenly seemed less daunting.

Bryn smiled and was about to stand to break up the hug-out when she heard the soft clop of feet coming down the hall. Helena pulled out of Rota's arms and wiped away her tears with her sleeve. She and Rota stepped farther apart.

Could it be Ashton? The brother who had zero posters on his walls and a wrestling mat set into his bedroom floor? Bryn was looking forward to meeting the boy to see why he was so different from every depiction she'd seen of a young human male.

"Come on, Ashton. Bryn is nice," Helena called out, her bright smile broad again, the resilience of youth blowing away the dark clouds as quickly as they had appeared.

Bryn climbed to her feet and straightened her clothes. She brushed back her hair and tried to smile through the swelling, touching her lips to make sure she wasn't bleeding. Not every human could stand the sight of blood.

She locked her gaze at Helena's level, expecting a boy about her height.

Then a head appeared. Long and positioned a lot taller than Helena's head.

And equine, not human.

Ashton was a horse. A very tall horse, at least seventeen hands tall.

Ashton stepped between Rota and Helena and paused, staring at Bryn, his huge nostrils delicately testing the air to take in her scent. He continued into the room and walked up to her, his brown eyes gentle with the wisdom of the ages behind them.

"This is Ashton?"

"That is Ashton. Not by blood, but my brother nonetheless."

"And this is his room?"

Ashton tossed his head as if nodding, before walking past Bryn and to his mats.

He stepped onto them, turned, and pawed like a dog making a nest before lying down with a heavy sigh, his eyes already half closed.

"He sleeps in here?" Bryn asked, knowing it was a stupid question but unable to stop herself.

"This is his room," Rota finally said.

"During the day?"

"Many of the horses sleep during the day," Helena said.

"Why?"

Helena opened her mouth to speak, but Rota touched her arm, silencing her.

"I am grateful that you stopped Helena from getting hurt. That buys you a few days to rest and heal. But as soon as you're able to leave, you're gone. Understand?"

"I can help you with the horses," Bryn said.

"I don't need your help, nor do I want one of your kind here." She pointed to the bed. "Get undressed and back in bed. You will not be wandering around, you will not be invited to eat with us, you will not be regaling my young friend here with fanciful tales. You will stay in this room, in this bed. Helena will bring you food and drink and any medications you may need."

"And Ashton?"

"The door will remain open so he can come and go. If you try to do the same, I will restrain you."

Bryn wanted to argue, she wanted to rail at Rota about loyalty and honor and obligation, but the woman was in no mood to listen, and, to be honest, Bryn was in no shape to belabor the point. Her body was already screaming to be horizontal; her eyes burned with the need to close.

"Am I allowed to use the bathroom, or are you going to provide me a chamber pot?" Bryn asked, unable to be meek in the face of Rota's edicts.

"Bathroom is right across the hall. Limit yourself to it and this room." Rota didn't wait for answer or argument. She turned away and left. "Helena. With me."

Helena flashed a smile at Bryn then disappeared.

Bryn sagged, her right hand braced on the desk while she took a few deep breaths, before removing her clothes. She slowly walked to the bed and climbed under the covers, the short stint on her feet having exhausted her reserves.

Yeah, there'd be no wandering, not for a few days at least. After that, she'd find a way to get Rota to accept her, listen to her. She burrowed deeper under the blankets and sighed, sagging into the mattress.

"Just so."

Ashton grunted.

Bryn looked at the resting horse, admiring his dark bay coloring, the perfect star on his forehead. Long lines, great bone. He had to be a warmblood, but she couldn't tell which kind, maybe Holsteiner. And he was older, probably over twenty years old, but in incredible shape.

"You going to help me win over Rota?" she asked the half-asleep horse.

He opened his eyes wider and studied her before lifting his tail and releasing a long, loud fart.

Bryn burst out laughing then gasped when her ribs protested. She wrapped her arms around her middle and smiled. "A champion fighter with a horse living in her house, with his own bedroom."

The Valkyrie had great affection for their horses, but nothing close to this. Ashton seemed to be more a member of the family than a tool for fighting. Were all of Rota's horses treated the same? The horsemasters who monitored the breeding, foaling, and raising of the horde's horses had a practical streak. Once a horse had proven it couldn't fly, or grew too old to fly, it was culled and sold to humans. Such horses were not allowed to take up space or use up resources that the next generation of foals needed to thrive and grow.

It wasn't ideal and even Bryn had regrets about some of the horses she'd cared for as an apprentice horsemaster. But that was the way it had been done for centuries, and the Valkyrie would not change. So, seeing Ashton, an older horse, still living with Rota—hell, living better than most of the Valkyrie—was jarring to put it mildly.

"What the hell happened to Rota? And what does it mean for the horde?"

7

Bryn opened her eyes to see Ashton standing over her, his lips an inch from her nose as he sniffed her. She held still waiting to see if he would do anything more, like try to eat her face for breakfast, but he did what he'd done for the last three days: He checked her out like a leering vulture then left the room for parts unknown.

Parts that Bryn had chosen not to explore while her body healed itself. Thank Odin for his gift of long, long life, great strength, and fast healing. Valkyrie might not be immortal, but it took a lot to kill them.

She sat up and evaluated her nearly healed injuries, pleased that the pain was almost gone. She threw back the blankets and swung her legs over the side of the bed. Yep, still some aches and pains, but agony had hit the road.

She stood and waited for the room to stop spinning before slowly walking to the bathroom. Time to test Rota's command to stay in the room. Bryn hadn't seen the woman since that first day, only Helena, who was kind enough to bring sustenance and a basin of warm water and a washcloth so Bryn could clean herself.

She rolled her shoulders then scratched the itch on her back. Ugh, a shower was in order.

The long hall was empty. She entered the bathroom and closed and locked the door out of habit. She started the water and waited until the room steamed up before she stepped into the large, square, tile-lined shower stall.

Hot water sluiced down her body from multiple shower heads. She sighed as she wet her hair and shampooed it, delighting in the volume of water beating her and the clean, pear scent of the shampoo and body wash. The only thing that could top the experience was an ice-cold, dark beer going down her throat and into her empty belly.

Refreshed, she dressed and combed out her long, silver-and-black-streaked hair, the large scar on her cheek flushed red from the hot water, making it stand out more than usual. Opening the door, she peeked down the hall again. Still deserted. She walked down the length of it until she reached a juncture.

The extra wide hall opened into a huge, two-story living space with a great room filled with deep, navy-blue sofas that invited you to curl up and relax with a cup of coffee, a fireplace formed out of pale stone, and to her left, an open kitchen with a large island that had a bar for eating. Beyond the kitchen, along the back wall of windows that looked out on the Colorado mountains, was a dark, wooden, rectangular dining table with benches and chairs.

To her right was the beginning of another wide hall; in front of her at the other end of the great room was a third hall that most likely led to more bedrooms.

The space was warm and comfortable and had that lived-in feel she loved. Nothing pretentious, nothing expensive—which was good considering Rota had a horse living with her—nothing you couldn't sprawl on.

So far, Bryn's luck was holding out; she hadn't seen Rota or Helena. Time to push a little more. She walked to the kitchen, opened the refrigerator, found a soda, and took it to hydrate and caffeinate.

Bryn looked at the two halls leading out of the great room and decided to skip the bedrooms—she could snoop around them later—and go for the stables. She wanted to see the horses, see if any of them could fly, and if yes, how many. Taking time to heal was fine, but it was time to move on with her reason for being here.

She eased to the corner of the hall and peeked around it. The passage was wide like the one to her bedroom, but it was longer, stretching between this barn-like home and the stables. At the very end of the hall was a wall of heavy, plastic strips hanging down, which you could push through yet still blocked cold or hot air from coming into the house.

She walked quickly to the strips, pushed them aside, and found herself in a huge barn with stalls that were the size of Ashton's bed. Much larger than the standard twelve-by-twelve-sized stall, and heaven for the horses. She turned left and went to the first door. Peeking inside she found a large, gray gelding lying flat, sound asleep on the same kind of black mats that Ashton slept on, with a small pile of shavings in one corner, like a designated potty spot.

During the morning. So odd.

She worked her way down all the stalls on this aisle, finding some horses sleeping and other stalls empty. The place was beautiful, pristine; each stall had its own tack room with leather halters and leads, brushes and combs and hoof picks, fly masks and boots.

In the back of each tack room were multiple feed bins for the various grains Rota fed each horse. A diet that was personalized, tailored to each horse's specific needs. Above each stall was a loft to store the hay, again with varying types for each horse.

Bryn touched a name plaque, letting her fingertips trace the letters carved deep into the wood. The barn was beautiful, and had taken a lot of work to build, and just as much to maintain. A spark of hatred formed in her heart at the bounty this one Valkyrie had when the horde was suffering so.

But that would be remedied soon, one way or another.

Laughter caught her attention. She dropped her hand and walked to a juncture in the stable. She turned toward the mirth that stoked her ire and strode to the double door opening at the end.

Morning sunlight streamed through windows high up the barn walls, blinding Bryn until she shifted to the left and hugged the minuscule amount of shadow by the door. She peeked around the corner and saw another wide hall that led to the indoor arena.

She heard muffled voices, but saw no one, so she ran down the hall and crouched by the entrance to the massive, open space, stalls lining the two long

44

walls. Rota had room for dozens of horses here, yet so many stalls were empty.

She inched along the deepest shadows hugging a row of stalls, avoiding the impossibly long fingers of sunlight that crept closer, stretching out to touch her, desperate to expose the intruder.

There she is, the liar, the oath breaker, breaking yet another promise.

Inside the arena, the roof soared stories high above her, much higher than the house or the barn, and extending much farther back than the others.

Bryn imagined horses flying in this space, like the now unused Valkyrie aviary, where the joyous sound of flapping wings, the beauty of a horse in flight, had long been absent.

Here there would be no concerns about bad weather, no worries that humans would see the miracle; you could fly day or night, free to do what nature and Odin had intended.

The pit of her stomach dropped. She swallowed hard against the stark images of starving Valkyrie and empty cribs that battered her.

Giggling caught her attention. She looked left.

Helena was trying to lunge a black, long yearling who had other ideas about what he should be doing with his time. He bucked and kicked, a fart exploding free with each effort, punctuating his exuberance, while Helena laughed all the harder, tears streaming down her face.

Bryn leaned out a little farther, risking the sun's desire to expose her, and saw Rota leaning against a wall, her arms crossed over her chest, the smallest grin breaking through her frown.

Some horsemaster, laughing when the colt should be disciplined for disobeying.

Before Bryn could decide whether to go back to the house or make her presence known, Ashton headbutted her in the back. She stumbled into the arena, tripped, and fell face first into the dirt. The once questing sunlight gripped her tight, illuminating her for Rota and Helena to see.

Rota slowly turned her head, her slight smile of a moment ago decimated by her scowl. "You're lucky I didn't ask him to stomp you."

Ashton walked past Bryn with what she swore was a smirk, on his way to Rota. He stopped next to her and pressed his head into her chest, groaning when Rota rubbed his ears then scratched his neck.

"Stomping was an option?" Bryn asked as she rose to her feet and brushed the dirt off her clothes.

"It's always an option for intruders and people who disobey my rules."

Helena called out for the colt to stop and slowly coiled the lunge line as she walked up to him. "Now, Rota, that's no way to treat your guest."

"She's not a guest."

Bryn lifted her chin and strode over to the pair. "Seems you're stricter with your 'guests' than you are with an unruly colt."

"He's still a baby, and his spirit is strong. I won't risk breaking it by being too heavy-handed."

Bryn spat on the arena floor. "Valkyrie horses are mighty and fierce; they must be trained with a firm hand, or they won't be willing to go into battle when we demand it of them. You've been away from the horde far too long if you've forgotten this."

Rota glanced at Helena. Bryn followed her gaze and stopped when she saw the girl standing stock still, her mouth open, her eyes glittering.

"Oh, please, don't stop on my account. I want to know everything," Helena said, a laugh bubbling up.

Rota pushed off the wall. "Alright, that's enough. Cool him down and put him up, Helena." She snapped her fingers at Bryn and pointed to the hall Bryn had come from. "You. Come with me." She marched past Bryn. "Now!"

Ashton nodded and flapped his lips as if laughing, then trotted after Rota, as if he couldn't wait to see what happened next.

"I'd hurry along, if I were you," Helena offered. "You don't ignore *the tone*."

Bryn snorted.

"Valkyrie!"

Helena's eyes widened and her smile faded.

Okay, crap. Maybe leaving my room wasn't the best idea.

Bryn turned and followed Ashton, wondering if she'd get a light touch or a heavy hand from Rota.

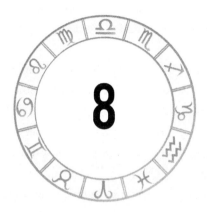

Rota marched, with Ashton behind her, all the way to the house. Bryn trailed after the horse, ignoring the intentional swishing of his tail.

"I've dealt with much harder cases than you, Ashton," she muttered.

He stopped swishing, lifted his tail, and farted.

"That's a warning by the way; he doesn't like to be crowded," Rota called back.

"He wouldn't kick me, not this sweet beast of a horse. We're sharing his room and we've come to an understanding."

Just as Bryn smirked, Ashton grunted and hopped his backend, a preamble to a kick.

"Don't be so sure, Valkyrie. I don't want you here any longer than necessary, and he knows that."

Rota stopped in the kitchen and pulled out a soda and a bowl of cut fruit.

Bryn stayed on the opposite side of the island. She was waiting for Rota to put the bowl down so she could get a handful when Ashton stepped up and Rota set the bowl down in front of him. She sneered at Bryn and walked into the living room, taking a seat and crossing her legs.

"Get a drink if you want one and join me. I will hear you out...once. Then you're gone."

Bryn opened the fridge, took a beer—it might be morning, but she needed to gird her loins—and sat on the sofa across from Rota. She slowly pulled the tab then took a long pull before crossing her legs and looking Rota in the eye.

"Start talking," Rota said.

No need to sugar coat it; Rota wasn't the type to suffer fools or prologues.

"The horde is dying," Bryn said. "The horses are almost completely gone."

"And you are here for..."

Bryn took another long drink, surprised that Rota seemed unmoved by her words. "I already told you. You need to come back and help us before it's too late."

Rota stood. "If that's it, get your stuff and leave. I've given you time to heal, I've fed you, I've tolerated your presence in my home. Get out."

Bryn finished her beer and set the can down gently to give her temper a chance to filter through her and dissipate. She slid back on the sofa and folded her hands in her lap. If Rota demanded she go now, without hearing her out fully, Rota would have to drag her out.

Didn't come this far and endure two beatings only to be shut out in less than five minutes.

"The Valkyrie, your sisters, need your help. I realize you had your reasons for leaving, but they can't be more important than the demise of an entire people... your people."

Rota stared down at her for a long beat before taking a seat again. "They broke their oath to Odin. That's why I left." She sat back in an imitation of Bryn. "Have they rededicated themselves to him?"

"No," Bryn snapped before taking a breath.

She really didn't want to go down that road.

"You do realize that by abandoning him they doomed themselves?"

Bryn closed her eyes for a moment. So, Rota wanted to go there. *Damn it.*

"Odin is gone. There is no rededicating to be done. He can't hear us, he can't answer us, he can't save us."

"Then why do you have that relic hanging on the leather thong around your neck?" Rota asked, pointing to Bryn's chest.

Bryn instinctively covered the piece of Odin's broken spear, Gungnir, with a hand, before reluctantly pulling on the thong until it appeared from inside her shirt. The priceless piece had been around Bryn's neck since birth. It had been bequeathed to her by her mother, and to her by her mother's mother, all the way back to before Odin fell, leaving the Valkyrie alone.

Bryn held it up and let the light reflect off the rune-covered metal. "This? It's just a trinket, something I found on my travels."

She tucked it back inside her shirt and looked up to see Rota smirking.

"Sell that to someone else, Valkyrie. You wear a relic around your neck and yet you still cling to the Valkyrie's disloyalty." She leaned forward and nailed Bryn with a stare that screamed challenge. "You want to help the horde? Go home. Make them rededicate themselves to Odin. Then, they will see a change in their fortune. Then, the horses will once again fly."

She stood and pointed to the hall leading to Ashton's bedroom. "Get your things and leave. There is nothing for you here."

Bryn's temper resurfaced. She jumped up. "I'm not leaving until you agree to come with me."

"I already beat you once. I'll happily pound you into the ground, cart your mangled body out, and dump you in the middle of nowhere for the wildlife to eat."

Bryn rested her fists on her hips and leaned forward. "It's going to take more than just you to accomplish that! Besides, you can't kill without Odin's approval."

Rota rounded the coffee table and bumped her chest against Bryn's, the two women tensed for a fight. "I don't plan on killing you. I'll beat so bloody you'll be begging for death when I dump you. The wildlife will do the killing."

The two women squared off, both fisting their hands.

"Rota!" Helena yelled as she ran into the great room, her phone in her hand. "Rota, something's happening at the house!"

Rota immediately turned away from Bryn, their argument forgotten, and just when Bryn had gotten her dander up to whoop-ass mode. She shook her hands to release some tension, and watched Rota and Helena put their heads together, murmuring about something on Helena's phone.

Helena swiped away tears, drawing Bryn's interest then a stirring of worry.

Rota took Helena's arm, nodded once, and they ran outside, Rota pausing for only a moment to grab a duffle bag out of a closet.

The minute Bryn saw that, she ran for her bedroom and grabbed her duffle, a near match in size to Rota's. All the Valkyrie had them. She sprinted after the woman and the girl, barely getting to the driveway in time to step in front of Rota's truck. She slammed her hand on the hood and stared at her estranged Valkyrie sister, until Rota bared her teeth and waved at Bryn to get in.

Bryn ran to the second-row door of the double-cab truck, flung the door open and leaped onto the seat as Rota gunned the truck down the gravel drive. She grabbed Rota's headrest and pulled her legs inside. Settling in her seat, she closed the door, if for no other reason than to make the annoying *ding-ding-ding* stop.

Rota and Helena said nothing. *Guess it's up to me to break the silence.*

She buckled in to keep her butt in the seat then leaned forward, looking first at Rota then at a pale and shaking Helena. "Someone going to tell me what's going on?"

"The alarm at Helena's home has been triggered and she got an alert on her phone."

"That's all? Crap, I thought we were going to war," she said, catching Rota's glare in the rearview mirror.

"Helena's parents are out of town."

"And? I hear an 'and' in there."

"And that means my brothers and their nanny are alone," Helena said, swiping at her tears.

"You sure they didn't set off the alarm accidentally?" Bryn asked.

"They know the code to turn it off," Rota said.

"They're not answering their phones," Helena added.

"Something's very wrong," they said at the same time.

Bryn sat back and unzipped her duffle, her adrenaline ramping up now that the pair's alarm was spelled out. "This happen before?"

"Rarely, but my parents have a nice house, so people sometimes try to break in."

Bryn could hear the tension in the girl's voice. She touched Helena's shoulder until the girl looked back. "It'll be okay. You've got me and you've got the Hulk here."

Helena sniffed. "The Hulk is a man."

"Rota could grind him into a great, green glob of goo, so that really makes her the Hulk, don't you think?"

Helena smiled through her flowing tears and nodded.

Bryn punched Rota's shoulder. "Right?"

"Punch me again and you'll find out."

Bryn sat back and opened her arms to the sides. "See? We got it handled."

That got a giggle from Helena. *My work is done.*

Rota turned onto an asphalt road, narrow, winding, vomit-inducing. She gunned it and the truck surged forward.

Bryn grabbed the armrest and braced herself. "How far is it to your house?"

"Fifteen miles using the Pass. A lot longer when it's closed," Helena muttered, her focus back on her phone.

"Everybody stop talking so I can concentrate, will you? Except you, Hel. Keep trying your brothers."

They remained silent for the rest of the trip, which was fine with Bryn, because she might have puked if she did anything more than concentrate on breathing. *In and out, in and out.*

"Valkyrie, are you with me?" Rota asked.

"Yes, I'm here."

"Good, because it's about to get bumpy."

9

Bryn opened her eyes just as Rota turned the wheel. The truck slid on gravel.

"Whoa!" Bryn yelled.

The truck bounced over the few small ruts in the mostly immaculate, gravel drive winding up to a thick stand of trees. Bryn grabbed the headrests and groaned involuntarily, partly because of the pain of being tossed around, partly because of her nausea.

"If you're going to puke, do it out the window!" Rota yelled, fighting the steering wheel.

Bryn curled her lip in defiance, even as she ground her teeth and stared at the horizon to keep her gorge down. "What's the plan?"

Rota came to a sliding stop far, far from the house. "Helena."

The girl opened the door and hopped out.

"You know what to do," Rota said, accelerating as soon as the door closed.

"Why'd you do that?"

"I don't want her in the line of fire. Plus, she's going to spur on the sheriff by telling him there's an intruder in the house and she's got a gun."

"Shouldn't they be coming out anyway?"

Rota pulled down a side road and flew through the tree-lined single track until she reached a barn style shed. She grabbed her duffle and threw it onto the passenger seat, then pointed to the long, padded bag under Bryn's feet. "Give."

"What are we doing?"

"You really want to help?"

"I'm here, aren't I?" Bryn said, handing over the bag.

Rota unzipped it and removed a rifle, followed by a scope.

"You're going to shoot them?"

"You got a problem with that?" Rota asked, her focus on her rifle.

"Not in the slightest, but I only have swords and daggers with me. You know, for real combat."

Rota left the truck, slinging the rifle over one shoulder and her duffle over the other. "You're not taking any of that."

"What?"

"I can't have you killing or maiming any human, not with the sheriff and his deputies coming."

Bryn slammed the truck door. "What do you expect me to do then? Battle-cry them into submission?"

Rota stepped into Bryn's space and sneered. She shoved a radio into Bryn's chest and held it there until Bryn gripped it. "I want you to go to the house and flush them out."

"With no weapons? Are you mad?"

"Fine. Take a dagger and hide it in your boot. That should be enough...since you're a Valkyrie."

"And what will you be doing? Are you going to kill them coming out of the house? Because I don't see how that's going to make the humans very happy. Or Odin for that matter."

"I'm not going to kill them, but I am going to send them a message they won't forget. Now go, get their attention and I'll be waiting to incapacitate them."

Bryn dropped her duffle, and just to piss off Rota she picked out two of the longest daggers that could be sheathed in her boots. She slipped one inside and kept the other in her right hand, the flat of the blade resting against her forearm to make it less obvious.

"Fine, but this buys me a few days with you, yes?" Bryn asked, her eyebrows raised as she waited for Rota to answer.

The woman didn't bother to look up. "If this helps Helena's family, consider yourself my guest. Until I say you're not. Got it?"

Bryn sprinted past Rota, her action being her answer. Just how a Valkyrie rolled. She pushed down her irritation with Rota and this half-assed plan so she could concentrate. She ran down the single track until it merged with the main gravel road, then slid to a stop when she saw the house.

Or mansion. The place was huge and fancy, a showplace of wealth and status, filled with cool, dark corners and empty spaces. Not a warm home that welcomed you to kick off your shoes and revel in family.

She rolled her shoulders back. "Fucking Rota. It could take a very long time to find these bastards, and there's too many places they can hide and pick me off."

Bryn squatted, studying the doors and windows, but saw no obvious signs of a lookout. A large, black Hummer sat in the circular driveway, and the front door was open. They'd walked right in, bold as brass.

Just ahead of her, a line of low hedges followed the curve of the drive. Bryn hunched down and ran to them, moving as fast as she could in a bent position until she reached them. She stepped over the greenery, ran to the vehicle, then raised her right arm and jammed the dagger into the back tire.

Hopefully they weren't the kind that could drive flat. Based on the rapid deflation, they weren't. Good. She trotted to the front tire and punctured it as well. At least the intruders wouldn't get away easily.

She eased around the front of the Hummer and watched the windows to the left and right of the door but saw nothing. No shadows moving back and forth. A glance at the other windows said the same. Whoever was inside didn't care about having a lookout, which was bad, or they were too stupid or inexperienced to think of it, which could be better, if they weren't the reactionary types who'd shoot first, ask zero questions later.

The one question that nagged was: With a car this fancy, why would they rob a house?

Bryn looked back the way she came and tried to see Rota, but the woman was too well hidden. *Here's hoping she doesn't shoot me by mistake.* She grimaced. *Or on purpose.*

Bryn stood and ran to the front door. She kept her back against the house and used the tip of her dagger to slowly open it, waiting for a shout or a shot. But no one noted the door moving.

She peeked inside and saw it was empty. And ridiculously huge. To the right and left were wide doors that opened into an office on one side and a feminine sitting room on the other. Both were unoccupied. Straight ahead the two-story foyer led to a curved double staircase. Beyond that, it looked like the house had an open floor plan.

Bryn slipped inside and ran to the opening of the great room, stopping to glance around for the intruders, but it was quiet, too quiet.

The back wall of the house was all windows, the view beyond spectacular. You could get lost in that view of mountains and valleys and small fields. You could breathe deep under that huge sky.

She took a deep breath of the wood floors and pine cleaner, and the rich scent of the heaps of flowers dotting the place. She shook her head. No one was down here; she could feel it.

Upstairs.

Taking the double staircase was a bit head on, so she ran into the kitchen and found a set of family stairs behind a door next to the pantry. She tiptoed quickly up until she reached the second floor. That was when she finally heard them.

Men, more than two; how many more she couldn't tell. They were looking for something and based on their whispered bickering, they were frustrated.

Whether it was a material prize or a human one she had no way of knowing. But if Helena's brothers and the nanny were hiding in the house, getting these men out had to be done now, before they were discovered, before shooting started if the men were armed.

She cracked the door open and peeked into the hall. Empty for now. She stepped out and closed the door behind her, took note of where the double staircase started—so far away, *yikes*—then started toward the sound of the men ransacking a room.

She stopped at the open door and eased her head over until she caught sight of four men hunched around a desk. Papers drifted through the air and landed on the floor; drawers were pulled all the way out then dropped on the carpet.

Two of the men glanced at the others and she silently groaned. Asshole and Idiot. Mr. C's sons and cohorts, the same men who'd scared Helena, and beaten Bryn senseless just days ago. Her fury shot into overdrive, her concerns about this mission combusting with a *poof.*

These guys sorely needed a lesson, and she was oh so very happy to give it to them.

She rolled into full view of the men and threw her dagger between them. It landed in the middle of the desk, the hilt quivering from the force of her throw.

The four jumped back with varying squeals, then whirled on her, their guns drawn.

"Shit!"

Bryn rolled out of range, her back against the wall. Plaster exploded inches from the right side of her head. She sprinted down the hall, her back hunched as far as it could go while still allowing her to run full out. *Rather take one in the ass than the back.*

The men yelled and the bullets flew, but thankfully she'd surprised them, so their aim was shite…at least for the moment. As soon as that moment passed, she'd be riddled.

She reached the stairs. Glancing back, she gasped. Damn they were close. She'd never be able to run down the stairs and out the door without making herself an easy target.

"Ahh!!!"

She grabbed the rail and vaulted over it, landing blessedly feet-first in the first-floor, marble foyer.

"What the hell?" one of the men shouted from the top.

Bryn didn't look back, oh no. She hotfooted it out of the house and took a sharp left, running toward Rota and the backup the woman was supposed to give her. That was if Rota was true to her word.

Shots rang out.

Fire exploded in Bryn's left arm and right hip. She staggered and lurched, saw the hedge ahead, and pushed through the pain. She needed to get behind it if she stood a chance of surviving; even a terrible shot got a bullseye occasionally.

Gravel flew up and stung her hands and face, but the bullets missed her. *Two bullets are enough, thank you.*

Bryn leaped over the hedge just as more shots were fired. Her right foot went numb and she crashed to the ground, rolling down an incline and into a stand of trees. She pulled herself behind the largest one and propped herself up. Why the hell hadn't Rota fired yet?

She leaned over and looked at the men. They had just reached the hedges and slowed, looking for her, when the distinctive sound of a rifle being fired washed over her.

Bryn watched Asshole go down. The other three glanced at him in bewilderment. *Come on, Rota, take them all out.*

No sooner had she thought the words than one, two, three shots were fired and one, two, three more intruders were down.

"Just so."

Bryn sagged, closed her eyes, and let out a sigh, waiting for the pain to set in. She wasn't getting up from this spot anytime soon.

The sound of tires speeding on gravel came up the drive. Rota got out of the truck and ran into the house. A few minutes later, she reappeared with two young boys and an older woman, the nanny probably, and led them to the truck. She spoke to them for a moment before she ran to Bryn.

"You going to lie there for the law to find?" Rota asked. "Or do you want a ride?"

Bryn held up a hand and shook it. "Hello. Bleeding here."

Rota pulled her to her feet.

"I think I've been shot," Bryn said, slurring.

"You need to run faster," Rota said, half carrying Bryn to the truck.

"Than a bullet?"

Rota grunted and opened one of the truck doors. "Move over, boys, you need to share."

Bryn cracked open an eye as Rota shoved her in. The boys were blond and blue-eyed just like Helena, and identical twins. They stared, their mouths agape as they took in her blood-soaked clothes.

"Wow, cool! You got shot!" one of the boys said.

The other boy backhanded his brother on the arm. "Doofus, she got shot three times."

"Cool," the boys said at the same time with the same reverent tone, both staring at the blood coursing out of the bullet holes.

Bryn gritted her teeth against the tsunami of pain that was drowning her.

"Glad to entertain," she choked out.

She pulled the piece of Odin's sword out of her shirt and gripped it with one hand, the words of a nearly forgotten prayer slowly coming to her.

"Can we touch the holes?" one of the boys asked.

Rota grabbed the back of his shirt—like a mama dog scruffing her pup—and plopped him into his seat without a word. Then she put the truck in gear and raced down the road, stopping only to pick up Helena.

The girl jumped into the passenger seat, sharing it with the nanny. She looked back at Bryn, her face white as a sheet. "You got shot?"

"Yeah, guess I'll have to stick around a while longer. Right, Rota?" Bryn asked.

Rota looked at her in the rearview mirror, her eyes narrowing. But all she said was, "Humph."

Yeah, I'm so in.

10

Bryn's grunts grew more emphatic with each piece of clothing Helena and Rota removed. "You didn't tell me that your house is the size of a football stadium."

"That's a gross exaggeration," Rota said.

"It's more like one and a half stadiums, actually. Or two, but who's counting?" Helena said, shrugging a shoulder before tugging on the ruined, bloody sleeve.

"Owww!"

"Oh, quit your crying," Rota scolded, cutting Bryn's pants off instead of trying to pull them over her injured foot. The one that had started bleeding again when her boot came off.

"Get me some of those nice drugs, why don't you?"

Rota snorted. "A Valkyrie needing pain medication? What would the horde say?"

"Right now I bloody well don't care what they'd say. I'm in pain...again...in the span of a few days."

Rota dropped the pants. "Fine, I need my med kit anyway. Helena, you okay to stay here?"

"I'm fine," the girl said quietly.

Rota left the two of them alone.

Bryn eased back on the bed, careful not to lean against the headboard. "Despite my bitching, I'll be okay."

"I'm sorry you got hurt helping my family."

"Helena," Bryn said. "Look at me."

The girl raised her head, her ever-present, sunny smile gone for the moment, in its place a trembling frown and tear-filled eyes.

"I'm fine, they're just flesh wounds. You know how fast I heal; I'll be up in no time."

"I just…" Helena said, her shoulders sinking. "I was so afraid for my brothers and you went in there without hesitating."

"Yes, and I'd do it again," Bryn said more sharply than she intended, ashamed that she'd bitched even for a moment about helping.

Helena was a good kid and she and her brothers were innocents. Bryn couldn't stand by and allow an innocent to be harmed. The world was cruel enough already.

Helena nodded, swiping at her tears. Bryn tried to sit up and couldn't stop a groan.

"Wait," Helena said, running to the door.

She returned with a couple of pillows, setting them on top of the stack of pillows already plumped up against the headboard. She paused for a long moment, silent.

"You okay, kid? I know it looks bad, but it's not." *Again, with the lying.*

"I wish my parents were here."

"How long have they been gone?"

"This time? Several weeks." Helena pressed a hand against Bryn's good shoulder. "Sit back," she said, guiding her.

Bryn sighed and closed her eyes. The pain, hot and stabbing in time with her heartbeat, blocked out everything around her, even the snoring Ashton.

Rota walked in, dropped the med kit, and pointed to the door. "Time for you to go, Helena. I can do this myself and your brothers need you."

60

"Of course, yes, I would imagine they're terrified."

Rota snorted. "No, they're climbing the walls, and any minute now they'll be crawling across the ceiling. I need to you to bring them down. Nan is the one freaking out."

"Home invasions and panic rooms aren't exactly in most nannies' job descriptions."

"I'd say not," Rota said.

Helena started for the door.

"Close it, will you?" Rota asked, though it came out more like a demand.

The girl slid the barn-style door closed, muffling the few sounds coming from the great room.

Bryn watched Rota set out the cleaning and bandaging supplies needed with swift efficiency. "Who the hell are they? These people who live in a massive mansion and leave their daughter with you and their sons with a nanny for days, for weeks?"

"They're friends I've known for a very long time. We look after each other."

"Is that how you can afford all this?"

Rota started cleaning Bryn's shoulder with not very gentle strokes. "Not that I intend to answer many of your questions, but, yes, Helena's parents lent me the money to buy the land and build all this. Though, I've already paid them back. I support this place on my own now."

"That's why you fight."

"I make a lot of money beating men to a pulp."

"You can't do that forever. You need a community around you, to support you, to keep this going long after you aren't able to."

"Like the horde?" Rota asked quietly as she selected a pair of long, curved forceps.

She held them up and nodded with a cruel smile as if affirming to herself that these would inflict the most pain possible while she fished out the bullets.

At least that's what the expression on her face screamed to Bryn.

"And why should I care about the horde after they turned their backs on Odin and their oath?" Rota asked as she pushed Bryn forward.

Bryn braced for the inevitable agony and she wasn't disappointed. The fire stole her breath and her ability to speak, the waves rolling through her until a soft sucking sound and a "voila" from Rota announced one bullet had been removed.

She fell back and panted, the black spots bouncing against the black edges around her vision. *I will not faint, I will not faint.*

She squeezed the covers tight and concentrated on inhaling and exhaling. *Okay, more like panting, but still in and out, right?*

"Oh, I forgot. You wanted some pain meds, didn't you?" Rota asked so sweetly that Bryn suspected the wretch would shit sugar cubes.

"What's a term that's worse than bitch?" Bryn asked between pants.

Rota set down the forceps and pulled a bottle out of the med kit. She handed Bryn two pills and a bottle of water. Bryn gave her a quick sneer, then concentrated on getting the pills down.

Cruel, cruel woman.

Rota crossed her legs and leaned back in the chair. "Let me know when you're ready."

Bryn closed her eyes again and concentrated on her oldest and most fond memories of her mother flying a horse. She'd been so young and couldn't wait to fly, but time had slowly stolen the ability from the Valkyrie, then started stealing their very lives. She had never flown a horse on her own, despite her failed, injurious attempts, but she had her childhood memories and her dreams.

Blessed heat and numbness began in her feet and worked their way up her body until she relaxed fully. She wanted to giggle but was too relaxed to push enough air out to make the sound.

"I'm ready," she said, slurring her words.

* * *

Like before, it only took days for Bryn to heal, but this time, she wasn't under orders to stay in her room. This time, Helena and her brothers, Alexander and Magnus, helped her into a wheelchair they insisted be rented so they could include Bryn in every meal, every excursion around the ranch. Or as many as could be reached in a chair.

But none of the explanations or assurances she'd overheard provided answers about the break-in. Mr. C's sons and friends didn't seem to need money, and the fact that they were rifling through an office instead of looking for valuables that could be sold off made Bryn wonder what the hell was going on. What were they looking for that could be more valuable than money, jewelry, or art?

Rota's smooth evasions spoke volumes; she knew what was at stake and she wasn't sharing. That piqued Bryn's interest. She would quiz Rota about the break-in, and the why of it, and soon.

More important than the break-in, knowing that the prickly Valkyrie cared about someone other than herself was good; something to use.

Bryn smiled to herself and basked in the morning sun, her belly sated, her pain mostly gone, and her heart full as she watched Rota work the horses. That was the greatest surprise of all: Rota's deep relationship with every horse under her care and the responses of the horses to her love. It took Bryn's breath away.

The Valkyrie horde had never loved their battle horses, though they did hold a deep respect for what the magnificent beasts could do in a fight, the sacrifices many a horse had made to protect the life of the Valkyrie on their back. There was a symbiosis, yes, and it was critical to both horse and warrior, but to call it love would be a stretch. Mutual admiration, mutual dependence, but not love, not like she saw in Rota's eyes, in her touch, in her every movement and manner around her horses.

They flowed, for lack of a better word. Horse and woman moved and communicated as one.

The difference between what Bryn had grown up witnessing and what she saw now was startling. It didn't change what she had to do, but it set up a longing in her that she wasn't sure she'd ever be able to get rid of.

"Bryn," Helena called out as she trotted over. She plopped onto the ground at Bryn's feet and placed a notebook on the ground. "How are you doing?"

Bryn turned her attention away from Rota and to the girl. "I think I'll try those crutches tomorrow."

"Wow, you do heal fast."

"Thought you'd figured that out."

"Yeah, but those were bruises and stuff. These are bullet wounds."

"Well, don't get any ideas that getting shot is no big deal, because it is. I heal faster than almost everyone, and I was lucky that those men had terrible aim. It's not like television, okay?"

"I know that. Not sure my brothers do, though."

Bryn laughed at the girl's exaggerated eye roll.

"Hey, Bryn, I wanted to ask you about something."

"Sure."

Helena scrolled through her phone for a second then held it up. On the screen was a photo of Bryn's back, bloody and swollen, her brand on full display. "What is that?"

Bryn stopped herself from recoiling. She wasn't ashamed of her brand or her numerous scars, but none were easily explained. Not to a teenage girl. "Why do you ask?"

"Because..." she said, pocketing her phone, "there are paintings of my ancestors in our house, and they have the same brand." She picked up her notebook, thumbing through it for a second. She showed a page to Bryn. "Your brand is part of my family crest."

Bryn stared at the crest for a long moment before she raised her head. "Rota!"

"I'm busy!" Rota snapped as she led a horse into the barn.

"Helena, can I look at your notebook while you get Rota for me?"

Helena stood and wiped the dirt off her jeans. She handed the notebook to Bryn, her expression puzzled, but she didn't question Bryn's request. "Okay."

Bryn waited for her to leave before she stared at the page again, taking in all the details in the crest. Irritation didn't quite cover the emotional turmoil bubbling up inside her.

She kept a finger on the one page as she flipped through the notebook, studying the girl's beautifully detailed drawings and reading her thorough notes. Helena had indeed done a lot of research into her family. A shadow fell on her.

She flipped the pages back to the crest and held it up. "Care to explain this?"

Rota crossed her arms and leaned back slightly, not out of defense, but defiance. "I don't have to explain a damn thing to you."

She snatched the notebook away from Bryn and closed it.

"Yes you fucking do!" Bryn scowled. "What are three members of the Aries royal family doing here in your house?"

11

ota walked away. Fury lashed Bryn, pushing her out of the wheelchair. She hobbled after the woman and grabbed her arm, jerking her around, much to Rota's surprise.

"Explain yourself," Bryn said.

Rota whipped her arm out of Bryn's grip and shoved her back, but not as hard as she could have. "I am honoring my oath to Odin to protect the Aries family, as the Valkyrie have done since Odin first proclaimed them to be the rulers of Midgard. Or at least until the horde broke their oath to the Allfather."

Bryn shoved Rota back. "The Valkyrie never, ever lived among the royals. We served them, protected them; we didn't wipe their snotty noses and teach them how to ride our horses!"

Rota growled at Bryn then leaned so close their noses almost touched. "*My* horses! Not *ours*, never *ours*. *Mine*." She stepped back and looked at Bryn from head to toe. "You're good enough to walk, you're good enough to leave. Be gone before

I get back to the house, or I will separate your head from your shoulders and mail it to Mr. C for a reward."

Rota marched away.

Bryn limped back to the wheelchair, collapsing into it, panting for a few moments until the dizziness was gone. She turned the chair and made her way to Ashton's bedroom.

"Damn right, I'm going to leave. There's nothing here for the horde," she muttered to herself as she threw her meager personals into the duffle on her lap. She pivoted the chair and stopped. "What do you want?"

Helena clutched her notebook tight to her chest. "You're leaving?"

"I'm no longer welcome."

She struggled to her feet and slung the duffle over her shoulder. Walking would be a bitch for a couple more days, but she had to get out of this place and away from the woman who had forsaken her duty to her sisters for an ancient, irrelevant oath given to a god who'd been trapped in Hades for centuries.

The stink of Rota's misplaced loyalty was too much.

"Can I come with you?" Helena asked quietly.

"Hell no."

Bryn pushed past the girl and slowly walked down the hall. She patted her jeans pocket and was happy that the car keys were there.

Helena ran past her, turned around, and walked backward, her palms up and facing Bryn. "You need a place to stay."

"Motel was fine before; it's fine now."

"You need help with your dressings."

Bryn stopped and gave Helena her best go-to-hell look. "Kid, I have made my way through far worse than this. A roll of duct tape and bar rags are all I need. What I don't need is you."

Helena pointed a finger at her and smiled. "*Supernatural!* I love that show."

Bryn shook her head. "Do your parents let you watch anything?"

Helena crossed her arms. "They're not home enough to stop me."

Bryn tried to walk past Helena, but the girl blocked her.

"You may not need me, Bryn, but I have mountains of questions and a huge, empty house."

66

"One that was just broken into for reasons no one has bothered to explain to me."

"Because I don't know why, and my brothers sure don't have a clue, but I do want to find out. We each have questions and we each have answers. Let's pool them."

Her blue eyes opened wide, and she smiled, bouncing on her toes.

The whole chipmunk-on-steroids look probably worked ninety-nine percent of the time for the girl, and damn if it wasn't working on Bryn right now.

"I won't stay at your house with your brothers; I don't want to be responsible for them. Or you for that matter. Besides, isn't your house a crime scene and off limits?"

"My brothers and Nan are staying here until my parents get back. That gives us a few days to find the answers we're looking for, and it gives you a nice place to stay until you're fully healed. As for the sheriff, he's already cleared the house for us to come back." She held up a hand and rubbed her thumb against her fore- and middle fingers, the universal sign for money. "Come on, what do you have to lose?"

"Helena!" Rota bellowed from somewhere in the house.

"I'll end up a pile of pulp if Rota finds out, and you'll be grounded until the day you die," Bryn said under her breath.

"Do we have a deal?" Helena whispered.

Bryn rubbed her face, the need to growl nearly overwhelming the need to stay quiet.

As frustrated as she was with Rota and the revelation that she was tight with the Aries family, Bryn needed to get her head out of her ass and remember why she was here. Getting kicked out of Rota's house and her life wouldn't help the horde, especially since she'd yet to learn whether Rota's horses could fly. Using Helena to remain close with hopes of reinserting herself could help her people. She liked the kid, but lives took precedence over a teenager's hurt feelings; she had to have continued access to Rota until she knew for sure whether the woman could help the horde.

Guess she'd have to risk the beating and deal with Miss Chirps-A-Lot for a while longer.

Bryn pulled the car keys out of her pocket "Get to the car, fast. I'll be there shortly. And for goddess's sake, stay out of sight."

Helena squeaked and jumped up before running out of the bedroom.

"Good luck, kid," Bryn said under her breath.

"Helena!"

Rota was almost at the start of the hall, so Bryn resumed her hobbling. Rota appeared then stopped.

"I know, I'm getting out of here as fast as my one and a half legs will let me."

Rota's eyes narrowed. "Have you seen Helena?"

"Not since I spoke with her earlier."

Rota crossed her arms and remained in place, staring, no offer to carry Bryn's duffle forthcoming.

Bryn gave the woman a tepid smile as she passed, continuing steadily because if she stopped, she was afraid she wouldn't be able to start again. "If I see her, I'll tell her you're looking for her."

"You do that," Rota said with a huff.

Bryn's rental car wasn't parked that far away, but this day it seemed to be miles from the house. She huffed and puffed her way to the sedan, curse words exploding out between each huff and each puff until she finally reached it and was able to collapse into the driver's seat.

Those darned black spots danced a jig, blinding her for a moment until she was able to catch her breath and her racing heart slowed.

"Took you long enough," Helena whispered, sprawled across the back seat. "I think someone peed back here."

Bryn dragged the duffel over her lap and dropped it on the passenger seat. She closed the door, started the car, and pulled out of the drive and away from Rota. "You won't suffer long; as soon as we're out of sight, you're driving."

"Yeah?" Helena chirped.

"You have a license?

"I already told you I have a learner's permit."

"Right, good, because I can't make it to your house without sending us over a cliff."

Bryn pulled over and they switched places. She lay down on the upholstered backseat and let the faint sweep her away. "Huh, does smell like pee."

* * *

"Time to get up, sunshine," Helena sang out.

The mattress bounced under Bryn. She cracked one eye and groaned. The wretch had opened every curtain in the room; the light was almost as glaring as Helena's grin

"Go away," Bryn groaned, dragging the king-sized pillow over her face.

"I made breakfast and you get to eat it in bed while I have mine over here at the table."

"What time is it?"

"Six o'clock and time's a wasting. Sit up, sit up! The sooner you eat, the sooner we can start our research!"

"Oh, mother of Odin! Why must you be so cheerful?"

"The better to wake you, my dear. Now sit up and eat."

Defeated by the incessant cheer, Bryn threw the pillow she'd used to cover her face across the room and pushed herself into a sitting position. She plumped her remaining pillows, of which there were a great number, sat back, and crossed her arms over her chest with a huff.

"Delightful," Helena said, placing the breakfast tray over Bryn's lap. She picked up the linen napkin by a corner and flicked it open before settling it over her. "And, voila," she said, removing the cover from the dish.

Bryn had to admit the fare before her was...staggering. Eggs and cheese, a Jenga tower of bacon, hash browns, toast with butter melted and dripping, jam, coffee, and sugar; there was enough here to feed all the warriors at a standard guard post.

"Well, go ahead," Helena said, waving a hand at Bryn's food as she walked to the table.

She uncovered her plate and Bryn nearly laughed. The girl had just as much food. "You really going to eat all that? I thought teenage human girls ate like birds."

Helena stacked three pieces of bacon and shoveled hash browns and eggs onto her fork, then into her mouth. "Just watch me," she said around her mouthful of food.

Bryn watched the girl eat like a linebacker in training, unable to keep up with Helena even though she was famished. "So how many siblings do you have?"

"Four. An older brother and sister, and you met the two banes of my existence."

"How much do you know about your family's history?"

"Immediate history, plenty. Further back, not so much." She leaned back in her chair and wiped her mouth with her napkin, her plate empty and so clean it looked like she'd licked it. "Today, I'm breaking into my father's vault, the one he thinks he's hidden so well."

"So you're a thief, are you?"

"Not at all. I'm not going to take anything, I'm just tired of being treated like a child. You are here, you are like Rota, and you are willing to answer my questions. The time has come for me to learn who I am."

Bryn finished her breakfast, the pleasant feel of a full stomach, the buzz of caffeine, and no small amount of curiosity making her amenable to the girl's machinations. "So, what first?"

Helena held up a finger and opened her notebook to a page with a long list. "For the sake of context, I want to start in the long hall. Then on to the hidden room."

She stood and straightened the table, putting plates and glasses and utensils on a large tray. She beckoned Bryn to do the same with a finger.

Bryn cocked her head, just for a moment, before shoving down her pique. The girl wasn't being bossy, didn't seem to be in her nature. What had become obvious was Helena's need for efficiency. So Bryn would tolerate her quirks and stow the irritation. It would be interesting to explore the Aries family history, some long-since forgotten, some idealized in song and story. The truth could be a boon for the Valkyrie and that's what she was always after. Anything to help the horde survive.

Bryn stood and tested her foot. Much better, good enough that she didn't need the crutches. "Lead on then."

Helena trotted to the door then bounced on her toes while she stood next to it waiting for Bryn to pass.

"It's going to be a long day, kid. Conserve your energy."

12

Bryn limped behind Helena, favoring her good foot and hip so she could stay on her feet longer, while they worked their way down a very long and wide hall with a white, marble floor covered by an impossibly long, navy rug.

"What is this room?"

"We call it the long hall, but it's actually the ballroom."

"With a rug?"

"Oh," Helena said with a laugh, pointing to a large, low box built into the wall at one end of the space. "We have a mechanism that rolls the rug up and stores it in that box thingy. When we aren't having a ball, this," she said, her arms wide as she twirled, "is the ancestral gallery."

She stopped spinning and pointed to the paintings filling the walls, paintings of the Aries family going back centuries. "The newest artworks are on the wall and open to the air; the oldest pieces are housed in sealed displays with controlled light, temperature, and humidity. Mom takes great care to preserve all this stuff. That's how Dad met her; she was an art restorer at a big museum in France. Really well known for it too."

Helena turned around and walked backward while she talked. "He convinced her to restore some pieces in his private collection and be a buyer for more. The rest, as they say, is history."

Bryn stopped at one sealed display; the painting looked ancient. In this depiction, as with all of them, the Aries blue eyes and blond hair showed through. Strong jaws, high cheekbones, the resemblance across the generations—including Helena and her brothers—was striking. There was no doubt that this was the royal line of the House of Aries.

"We look alike, don't we?" Helena asked.

"Eerily so. The Aries genes are strong."

Helena smiled, taking the statement of fact as a compliment. "I wanted you to see this first so you would have no doubt about who we are, who I am."

Bryn walked down the hall until she reached the portrait of Helena's parents. She studied it, seeing the girl in both. "I haven't doubted that from the moment you showed me the crest."

Helena sighed, as if a weight had been lifted. "Good." She curled a lock of her hair around her finger. "And you are a Valkyrie, like Rota?"

Here we go. "Yes."

Helena nodded once and relaxed. "Okay. Now that the bonafides are out of the way, follow me."

The girl walked through the closest door and started down another long but much narrower hall in a separate wing of the house. She opened a wide door and ushered Bryn into a house-sized master bedroom.

"Your parent's room is all the way across the house?"

"Oh, yeah. They carry on like rabbits," Helena said, shuddering. "The rest of us are thrilled we live far, far away."

She beelined it to the bathroom, Bryn right behind her.

Bryn stumbled to a halt next to a marble Roman tub with the requisite columns. The extravagant bath could seat several people. "Holy crap."

Helena joined her. "Right? When I was little, I pretended I was a mermaid. Fun times."

"And nothing like a ram-head faucet to scream, 'I am Aries,'" Bryn said under her breath at the sight of the fixture.

Helena grabbed her arm and pulled. "I don't know how much gawkage you have stored up, but don't waste it on this. I suspect there's going to be plenty to gawk at in the basement."

She pulled Bryn away from the tub and led her into the back of a large walk-in closet lined with men's clothes and shoes.

"This is their closet?" Bryn asked, looking around the huge room.

"Not theirs, his. This is Dad's bathroom. Mom has her own."

"Odin help me," Bryn muttered as she turned slowly.

Helena stopped at a full-length, ornately framed mirror taking up a section of wall. She ran her fingers down the right side until, with a *click*, the mirror opened slightly.

She glanced over her shoulder and smiled. "Come." Pulling the frame open, she stepped onto a long, narrow landing large enough to hold four people comfortably. She flipped on a light. "Shut the door behind you."

Bryn did as the girl asked, pulling the door until it latched. "So, this leads to a safe?"

Helena started down, her white-blonde ponytail bouncing, her gangly, coltish legs chewing up the stairs.

"You'll see," she said, her voice ending on a peak.

Bryn rolled her eyes. She'd never met someone so excessively happy that they ended their sentences on an operatic high note. *May I never be so blessed again.*

They worked their way down the stairs, the air cooling rapidly the deeper they went. Finally, they reached the end and found a tall, narrow, nondescript, metal door with a keypad to the left.

"This is as far as I've gotten in the past. Today, I'm opening the safe room itself," Helena said, flipping on a light.

"What held you back?"

"Opportunity, knowledge, and," she grinned at Bryn, "a partner who is a Valkyrie like Rota but without Rota's pesky sense of right and wrong."

Bryn snorted, but she couldn't fault the girl's thinking. Damn clever human.

"Wait. Why do you need a Valkyrie?" she asked, not sure she wanted to know the answer.

Helena pulled two small packets out of a box attached to the wall. She handed one to Bryn. "Tear it open, clean a finger."

"I'm not going to like this, am I?"

Helena ignored the question. Instead, she cleaned her left forefinger with the alcohol gauze then pressed the fingertip into a dip in the plastic below the keypad.

She hissed then backed away, pressing the gauze against her finger, smiling at the small, green light. "Good."

"What was that?" Bryn asked.

"Access to the vault," Helena said. "Or at least my part."

"How do you know all this stuff?"

"I listen. Adults say the most incredible things when they think you're not paying attention." She gestured to the keypad with both hands. "This requires the blood of my father alone, or Rota alone. But," she pointed a lone finger up, "if you have a blood member of the Aries family and a Valkyrie, who are not are my father and Rota, you can still get in. You just have to have one of each or it doesn't work."

"So that excludes your mother?"

"She doesn't care about that," Helena said, waving a hand. "She's more concerned about protecting what's inside and if that means she can't just rando walk in, well, that means more security, which she's all about." She put her hands on her hips. "So, are you going to do this or what?"

Bryn ripped open the packet and cleaned her left forefinger. "Kid, this better be good."

She pressed her fingertip into the shallow-cupped well. Just when she thought nothing would happen, a sharp sting startled her. She grunted and pulled her finger away.

"Why do fingers hurt so much?" she asked, not expecting an answer, as she flapped her hand.

Helena leaned forward and bounced on her tiptoes.

"Please don't squeal," Bryn said.

"But this is so exciting."

"Squealing hurts my brain, kid."

The green light flashed.

"Yes!" Helena said, opening her mouth, pre-squeal.

"Ah, nope. I said no squeal."

Helena nodded as she danced in a tight circle before pulling a piece of paper out of her pocket and typing in a code. The door opened with a hiss. "We're in!"

Bryn grabbed the edges of the door and pulled it open, letting Helena enter before turning her attention to the cavernous vault. She stilled. Her heart flopped hard once then started beating fast.

She stepped up to the first long, wood and glass cabinet and studied the weaponry protected within. The shields and axes and maces and swords were old, back to the time of the first Vikings and the Norse gods and goddesses of old. And they were locked away in a cabinet in a deep, dark hole in the ground, guarded by humans.

She gently pressed a hand against a pane of glass and leaned close to see the exquisite carvings and etchings; names and animals and deities and runes covered each weapon. The craftmanship stole her breath away, as did the ancient, black blood still encrusted in crevices and notches.

Stepping back, she counted the cabinets. "Are they all filled with weapons?"

Helena did a three-sixty, her head craned back to look at the shelves and cases of treasures. "It looks like some have clothes; some have books. They're all ancient. I don't know how my family came to be in possession of all this. I mean, my family is rich, so we could afford to collect it, and our ancestors came from Norway, so there's the possible reason to collect. Though there's not a lot of Norse stuff upstairs."

"It's a puzzle," Bryn said.

"One I hope you'll help me solve," Helena said, a question unasked in her glance.

Bryn walked away rather than answer the question. She was here, wasn't she? There was so much she could tell Helena, but should she? What exactly would be gained by telling the girl the whole truth? It's not like she would ever become a queen, or a Valkyrie, for that matter. Of course, dangling the truth would be a way to get the answers and cooperation Bryn sought. A little bit of the truth could gain her far more than she gave out.

Bryn took her time studying the priceless relics, working her way around the room until she came to the wall opposite the entrance. In the center of the shelves stood a door, a keypad to its right. To her right, another line of cabinets and display cases.

But the door drew her interest and held it. "You know how to open this?"

Helena stepped up to the pad and pulled out a piece of paper. "My parents are very smart, but they underestimate their children—Mom not as much as Dad, though—even with all the trouble we've gotten into."

She typed in the code and the light turned green. She pushed the door latch down and the door opened with a hiss. "They also made the mistake of tormenting us at Christmas by creating novel codes for our presents every year. It was up to us to break the code so we could each open one gift on Christmas Eve."

She glanced back at Bryn.

"And you always broke the code first."

Helena grinned and nodded once.

Bryn saw the twinkle in the girl's eye. "But you never let anyone know it was you, did you?"

"Nope. I made sure to lead them there so one of the others solved it."

"Clever."

"Always good to hold something back," Helena said, tapping a finger against her temple. "You ready?" she asked, her hands on the door.

Bryn nodded instead of rubbing her hands together; that might have been a bit much.

Helena pulled hard and opened the door wide. Lights blinked on, obviously tied to the opening of the door, revealing another huge room.

"Holy shit," Bryn said, the words drawn out.

Helena walked inside, craning her neck to look at the tall ceiling. "This is unbelievable."

Bryn followed the girl and immediately understood what she meant. Like the other room, the walls were lined with dozens of shelves filled with books; some of the books even had chains attached. A long line of tables, two by two, started a few feet in front of them and continued for yards. You could seat every Valkyrie in her horde at these tables and have room to spare.

Beyond the tables were more wood and glass cases; where the shelves ended the tall cabinets began. There had to be hundreds of them.

Bryn started down the left side; Helena took the right.

"How rich is your family?" Bryn asked, her fingertips tracing the gold leaf on the spine of one book.

"Richer than even I knew. This is crazy."

"There are centuries' worth of books here," Bryn said, moving more quickly to reach the cases and cabinets.

They were locked, but the glass revealed the treasures stored inside. Weapons and armor, pottery so old that the paint decorating them had faded. There were plates and mugs, coins and jeweled crowns, the centuries-old wealth of the family stored away from the world.

Bryn looked farther down the space. "What else do you have hidden away?"

Ignoring Helena's occasional gasp, Bryn worked her way down the rows until she reached the end, and another door.

Metal, formidable, this one didn't have a keypad; instead, there was a small square with a glass screen.

Helena studied it for a moment. "Finger scan, I think."

"It's not going to have either of our prints."

"Maybe." She flashed a grin. "Doesn't hurt to try."

Before Bryn could stop her, Helena placed her right thumb on the pad and pressed down. "Hmm—" she said before jerking her hand back. "Ouch!"

A small needle in the center of the glass pad retracted into the hole Bryn hadn't noticed before.

"Did you get stuck again?" she asked Helena.

The girl held up her thumb. "Yeah, it took more blood this time."

"Well, that can't be good," Bryn said, looking around the space, wondering when the alarm would go off.

But another hiss of escaping air announced the opening door.

This time, the lights that came on were much dimmer, more like you'd expect in a museum. The hairs on Bryn's neck rose. She wasn't easily spooked but something about this room had her on edge. Before she could take Helena's arm and pull her away, the girl disappeared inside.

"Damn it."

Bryn rolled her shoulders, forcing her trepidation down. *Get in, see what's locked away in a vault inside a vault inside a vault way underground, then get the hell out.*

13

The air was colder in here; the humidity felt low. A small, wooden table sat to the right with a pair of chairs tucked in. More shelves lined parts of the walls, but there were far fewer books; these must be the most precious in the Aries family collection.

Helena stayed still until Bryn stopped next to her.

"What's this?" the girl asked.

"The rarest of the rare, I'm assuming."

Helena slipped her hand into Bryn's like a child might do a parent, seeking reassurance. Not something Bryn would have normally allowed, but the girl's hand was cold and sweaty. She was frightened, truly scared.

Bryn squeezed her hand. "Let's take a quick look then get out of here."

"Okay."

"Want to stick together this time?"

Helena released Bryn's hand but remained next to her, nodding. "Yes."

Bryn inclined her head to the left and they walked together to the shelves. These books were enclosed in a temperature- and humidity-controlled case. The books appeared to be very old, even older than the books in the larger room, which kind of blew Bryn's mind. Either that or they were locked away because they were dangerous, something humans didn't understand or appreciate.

If she was reading the worn, gold words embossed on the spines correctly, these were books of magic. She stopped at one. Black magic.

Bryn looked across the much smaller room then crossed it and read a few of the spines. "White magic."

No wonder Aries had hidden them so deeply and so well. Any number of witches and sorcerers would kill to get their hands on these books. A chill gripped Bryn and it wasn't from the temperature of the room.

"I wish I could take one of these out to figure out why they're locked away," Helena whispered.

"I think we've done enough investigating today. Let's not push it," Bryn said. *Let's not unleash a plague or three or call down evil,* she thought.

"One pass through then we go?" Helena suggested.

"Let's."

They walked slowly, taking in the books as they went.

"My parents have a lot more secrets than I thought," Helena said.

"I suspect most parents do. It's not a bad thing, protecting your children."

"I guess, but this…this is going far beyond protecting us. I thought exploring this place would be like using a genealogy site—see who your family was and what they did."

They reached the back of the room and stopped next to a wooden pedestal with a black, leather-bound book on it. Bryn laid her palm on the book, surprised that there was no writing on the cover.

Helena crouched and touched the back wall. "This isn't original."

Bryn opened the book and squinted to see the writing in the low light. "Uh-huh."

"I think this is a false wall. Something's behind it."

"We'll go in a minute," Bryn said, mumbling as she leaned closer to the text.

Helena duck-walked around the edges of the wall.

"What are you doing?" Bryn said, finally noticing the girl's strange movements.

"I've found…"

Helena pushed on a small piece of stone and the false wall shifted, a pale blue light and fog escaping around the edges.

Bryn abandoned the book for the new discovery. "What the hell?"

They gripped the top edge of the false wall and pulled it to the side.

Before they were done, a huge, rectangular box slid out of the wall, like it was on wheels. At least eight feet long, the futuristic-looking tomb was made of metal. There was no window to see inside, only a handle to lift the lid.

Bryn and Helena looked at each other for a second.

"What do you think this is?" Helena asked.

"I have no idea."

Helena's eyes glittered. "We probably shouldn't open it."

Bryn shook her head slowly. "Definitely shouldn't."

They said nothing for a long moment, then Bryn gripped the handle and released the lock. More light shone around the edges of the lid; more cold fog jetted out.

"Whoa," Helena said, her voice a whisper.

I really should be the adult here. Stop snooping and leave. Listen to my rising hackles and back away.

"One look then we go," Bryn said, surprising herself.

She heaved open the heavy lid and rested it against the wall then waved her hands over the fog-filled opening until a shape emerged. The very large shape of a tall, blond, muscular man.

"Is he frozen?" Helena asked, reaching out to poke him. "Whoa," she repeated, leaning closer. "Is he naked?"

Bryn grabbed her wrist and pulled her back. Her earlier sense of foreboding had been realized.

"No touching. And no ogling the naked man," she said, trying to wave the escaping fog back over the man's rapidly appearing, supersized genitals.

When that didn't work, Bryn pushed Helena farther away and out of view of that which no teen girl needed to see.

"What's going on?" Helena asked. "My parents have a frozen stiff in the basement? Who does that?"

Bryn held up a hand to make Helena stay put, before returning to the man and leaning close to get a better look at his face. "I don't think he's dead."

"Seriously?"

Helena joined Bryn again, the hand signal not enough to stay a curious girl. Luckily, more fog had drifted around the man, so he was decent again. Helena stood next to Bryn, their shoulders touching, peering at the man's face.

Reaching into her back pocket, she pulled out her phone and took several pictures. "That's just too creepy."

"And none of your god-damned business!" Rota bellowed from behind them.

Bryn and Helena jumped and split apart.

Rota marched up to them, the rage that enveloped the older Valkyrie an invisible force so palpable it sent Bryn scrambling backward until she hit the pedestal holding the book. Bryn grabbed the stand before it fell but the book hit the ground with a *splat*.

"Helena Frigg Aries! Your curiosity has led you too far this time!"

"Frigg? Your middle name is Frigg?" Bryn asked.

Rota stopped stalking over to Helena and slowly turned her head to Bryn, the scowl deepening and widening until it was a great chasm of wrath and loathing with a big heaping promise of retribution.

Bryn shut her mouth with a *snap*.

"How did you know we were here?" Helena asked, her concern tempered by her curiosity.

Rota turned her full attention on the girl and held up her phone. "I got a call from your father. Want to know what he said?"

Helena audibly gulped. Seemed the girl had the sense to finally recognize the terrible trouble she was in.

"There's an intruder?" Helena asked, her voice shifting to stratospheric by the end.

Rota took a deep, deep breath. "There's a break-in, Rota. In *the* vault." She reached around to the small of her back, pulled out a gun, and held it, her arm relaxed by her side. "You know what else he said?"

Helena shook her head instead of speaking.

Rota closed her eyes, her free hand slowly closing into a fist. "Take care of it. You know what to do."

"He asked you to kill?" Helena asked, her voice barely audible now, her face bone white.

Rota opened her eyes again. "Get out."

"But—"

Rota slipped the gun into the small of her back. She took Helena's arm and pulled her forward, out of the room. "Valkyrie, close the lid and come with us."

Bryn almost nodded. Hell, she almost fell to her knees and begged for forgiveness, and that wouldn't do at all. But there was no logic in aggravating the already monumentally pissed-off woman. She hustled over to the box and closed the lid. The moment the release clicked, the coffin or deep freezer slid silently back into the wall, and she closed the false wall behind it.

She had started for the exit when the book on the floor caught her eye. She picked it up and meant to place it back on the stand, really, she did, but her fingers squeezed it tight. Bryn glanced at Rota's back then quickly tucked the book inside her pants, making sure her shirt covered the theft.

"Valkyrie!"

"Coming," Bryn said, sounding like a child answering her mother.

She closed the door behind her, almost gratified to hear the lock engage, before trotting after Rota. They left the library slash exhibit room and closed and locked that door as well. Only then did Rota release Helena.

"Since you can't be trusted not to stick your noses where they don't belong, you're both coming back to the ranch."

Bryn shrugged. Helena skipped ahead and turned to walk backward, a huge smile on her face.

Odin help us. The girl is irrepressible.

"You were really going to shoot me?"

"Once I saw it was you, no. Your parents, god only knows why, are fond of you."

"You were going to shoot someone, though."

Rota stopped. Bryn almost ran into her.

"After what you saw in there, do you have any doubt that I would?"

Helena cocked her head. "What, exactly, did I see? Who is that man? Why is he frozen? Is he dead, or in suspended animation?"

82

Her wiggling fingers made it all seem so ridiculous.

"Ohhh," Helena said, gasping. "Do you think Mr. Caldwell's sons were trying to get down here?"

Ridiculous, if Bryn didn't have the same questions and many more. The pressure of the book against her back reminded her that she might have the source of at least some of the answers.

Rota lifted her arm and pointed behind Helena. "Go."

Helena squealed and jumped in the air. "This is so exciting!" She took off at a run. "I'll get my things." She spun around when she reached the base of the stairs. "Better grab a drink. You're going to need it for all the talking you're going to do."

Bryn watched the girl disappear. "She's gone. What the hell is going on?"

Rota spun on one heel and hit Bryn square in the chest with the palm of her open hand. Bryn staggered back and hit the wall.

Rota stepped into her, almost nose to nose, one hand loosely gripping Bryn's throat. "You will stay away from her, her family, and this house, get me?"

Bryn pushed against Rota; the women struggled in silence.

"I do what I want," Bryn said, pressing the gun she'd lifted from Rota under the older Valkyrie's chin.

"Clever hands, but you aren't going to pull that trigger, any more than the Valkyrie are going to follow you here and try to steal my horses."

"I don't know, you're a world class asshole. It might be worth it."

"You do that, and the horde will never fly a horse again."

Rota shoved against Bryn as if making a point before stepping back and holding out her hand.

Bryn tilted her head and sneered. "I don't think you've had any more luck than we have at finding a horse that will fly."

Rota shook her hand, the demand for the weapon silent, yet still loud. "Wanna bet?"

14

Bryn hustled to Rota's truck as fast as her complaining wounds and bruises would allow, Helena behind her carrying both of their bags.

Adrenaline had given her the strength to move quickly; hope had dulled the pain. Two words, two, and everything she'd done—everything she'd suffered—had been forgotten; her every dream had come true. "Wanna bet?" was all it took to fill her with a renewed sense of purpose.

Odin himself can't help Rota if her taunt is a lie.

Bryn climbed into the truck, gripped the relic hanging around her neck, and silently mouthed her favorite prayer to the Allfather before she realized what she was doing. What was it about this place and this old Valkyrie that had her seeking solace when she hadn't done that since she was a young child? This place—this situation—was turning her upside-down and that couldn't be tolerated.

She pressed her lips together to stop the prayer and released the relic.

Helena climbed into the back and Rota took off down the drive, scowling and clenching the steering wheel.

"Your parents are cutting their trip short. You're to stay with me until they return."

"Uh-huh," Helena said.

Bryn glanced back and saw the girl had gone from sunny to a teen pose: arms crossed and scrunched in her seat, moments away from a pout if the dark expression on her face told the tale. Mercurial defined.

"I have a right to know what goes on in my family," she finally said, the pouty mood shifting to defiance.

I could get whiplash from the rapid changes.

Bryn looked at Rota. This could prove to be interesting if Helena could keep Rota talking.

Rota glanced in the rearview mirror. "No, you don't. Your parents decided to keep this from you, a decision they made long ago for reasons that are none of your business unless they deem it so. You chose to ignore this and have risked much because of it."

Helena sat up and scooted to the edge of her seat, her hands gripping the headrests as they bumped down the road. "What have I risked?"

"You have a phone. Call your father and ask him."

Bryn relaxed back and rolled her eyes. *Damn good diversion.*

Helena, however, didn't give up so easily. She pulled out her phone and scrolled through it for a second before showing Rota the screen. "I don't have to call father because it can only be about the popsicle."

Rota grabbed her phone and slammed on the brakes. The truck shuddered to a stop and Rota immediately deleted the photo and all the rest that Helena had of the man and the secret rooms. Then she tossed the phone back to Helena and began driving again.

Bryn's jaw dropped, as did her heart. That was the only evidence of what they'd seen.

Helena laughed and sat back. "Oh Rota, deleting the photos from my phone doesn't delete them from the cloud." She snorted. "I can access them anytime I want."

"Crow now, while you can. Your father will be interested to know what you have done." Rota heaved a sigh. "It's really too bad. Your riding was coming along too."

Helena's face paled and she crossed her arms again, but this time the defiance was gone, replaced by tears. "You don't mean that."

Bryn could have sworn she heard the crack of a whip. Hormones were a bitch.

"It's the second thing your father ordered. No riding. You can do chores or stay inside with your brothers and Nan until they're back."

Silence ruled the road all the way back to Rota's.

The moment the truck stopped, Helena jumped out, her bag in hand, and ran inside, slamming doors as she went. Bryn pulled her bag out and winced at the weight of it. She kept her mouth closed as she trudged behind Rota into the house.

"Same room, same rule. I don't want to hear or see you," Rota ordered, pointing down the hall to Ashton's bedroom.

"What about the demonstration? I want to see if you have a horse that can fly."

"No. And that you think you have the right to demand anything from me after what you and Helena did makes that a hell no."

Rota stormed to the kitchen, her back to Bryn.

Conversation over.

Bryn hesitated for a moment then walked to her bedroom. She dropped her bag with a sigh and closed the door despite this being Ashton's room. As much as she had learned at the Aries house, it had generated a buttload more questions and blown her chance to see if Rota's horses flew. She heaved another sigh; not the most productive day.

She kicked off her shoes, climbed in the bed, and pulled the covers up high, the book she'd taken from the manscicle's room making itself known. She pulled it from the small of her back and held it between her palms for a moment; hopefully it had some answers. Opening the cover, she read the title written long ago: *A Treatise Of The Monstrum: The Origins Of The Black Zodiac.*

* * *

Bryn finished the book and hid it under her mattress for the time being. She rose into a sit, took a long, deep breath, and let it explode out of her chest. She had no idea who had written the treatise, they never listed their name, but whoever wrote it was less important than what the book revealed.

The Twelve, the former human princes who had become the rulers of the subterranean paranorm world called the InBetween, had sanctioned the creation of a secret group of men called the Black Zodiac, the collective known as the Monstrum. Dates weren't mentioned, but because the Zodiac Assassin Lyon *was* mentioned, she surmised that the Black Zodiacs had been created around the same time as the known Zodiacs. The main difference was the Black Zodiacs were never revealed, much less allowed to roam free.

According to the author of the book, when the Twelve had realized the evil that they had created with these new, much darker Zodiacs, they had covered it up by separating the Black Zodiacs and sending them to parts unknown. The men had been disappeared.

How the Aries family, humans, had ended up with the Aries Black Zodiac was a mystery only Helena's father could answer.

"You can be damn sure I'm going to ask him," she said to the empty room.

She stood and took a mental inventory of her aches and pains. Not bad. The rest had done her good physically, even if the book had disturbed her mentally. The time for more answers would arrive with Helena's father, but while learning about the Black Zodiac in Aries's possession was interesting in a gut-clenching, nauseating kind of way, it wasn't relevant to her mission or the Valkyrie's needs. She couldn't allow herself to be distracted.

She walked to the closest window and pulled back the curtain, confirming what she already suspected. The sun was falling behind the horizon.

A soft tap on her door brought her out of her ever-deepening funk. "What?"

The sliding door opened slightly, and Helena stuck her head inside.

"Hey," she whispered. "Rota has gone to the arena."

Bryn turned, crossed her arms, and leaned against the windowsill. "So?"

"So, I know a place you can watch the horses without her seeing you. You do still want to watch them?"

"You know I do, but you also know that I'm inches away from being kicked off the ranch."

Helena rolled her eyes so hard Bryn was surprised the girl didn't hurt herself. "And I'll be stricken from any horse time, even mucking stalls. Live a little."

Bryn snorted at the audacity and ignorance of the statement. The girl had no idea what living was like, but if she was correct…

"You're absolutely sure we won't get caught?"

"Positive. Trust me."

Bryn couldn't believe the horde's existence was hinging on a teenager's promise, but she had to see the proof, if there was any. "Okay."

"Great room."

Helena's head disappeared along with the rest of her.

Bryn changed clothes and slipped on her boots. Time to see what the renowned horsemaster turned traitor to the horde had accomplished in the past few years. If Rota's hinted claim was bunk, Bryn wasn't sure what she could do to save the horde.

A soft *clop-clop* sounded down the hall. Ashton was coming and he'd expect to access his room. She opened the sliding door and poked her head out. The dark bay horse stopped when he saw her, bobbing his head and twitching his lips as if impatient for her to come out.

"Alright, I'm coming."

Bryn left the room and walked up to the huge gelding, admiring his gorgeous lines and coloring and the intelligence in his big, dark eyes. She reached him and pressed a hand against his neck.

He snorted but let her touch him.

She stroked the silky coat. "Did Rota send you to spy on me?"

As if to refute her comment, he turned away from her.

Bryn backed up a few steps to give the horse room to turn around, then watched him go down the hallway leading to the barn.

Helena *psst-ed* and waved at Bryn to join her.

Bryn crossed the great room, following the girl into Rota's bedroom and to the closet. Inside, Helena rose up on her tiptoes and pulled on a cord suspended from the ceiling.

"The attic, what there is of it," Helena whispered. "These barndominiums keep the roofline open but I think Rota stipulated that there be access to all the buildings along the tops of them."

"It's smart to have more than one way to get to the horses," Bryn commented, following Helena up the ladder and into a crawl space so tiny it was almost literally a crawl space.

Bryn bent at the waist and pulled up the ladder behind them.

A light switched on, breaking through the sudden darkness. A narrow walkway was ahead of them, ending in a right turn that sent them over what Bryn thought was the third bedroom. If she was correct, the walkway should go left at any moment…

Sure enough, they turned left and walked on.

"Are we over the hallway that connects all the buildings?"

"Yeah."

Helena stopped at a door and opened it.

Bryn held up her hand to block the light. They were standing on a walkway tucked in at the roofline, high above the stalls.

Helena headed left. "The walkway goes all the way around the barn and the arena."

"What's that set of stairs for?" Bryn asked, pointing across the barn.

"They go to the cupola at the very center. There's another set up ahead." Helena trotted away. "Hurry or we'll miss it."

15

Bryn followed Helena around the barn, through the darkness of the passage between the barn and the arena, and up a steep set of stairs that seemed to go on forever, before opening a door and stepping out into the light again. The walkway narrowed even more inside the arena, so tight against the roof that Bryn and Helena had to bend at the waist again to follow it.

Unlike the barn, this walkway was more enclosed; from the ground it would be nearly impossible to see them. Bryn slowed and peeked over the waist-high wall.

Rota stood in the middle, watching several horses prance and snort around her.

Bryn watched the woman with her charges, watched how Rota studied each horse, how she smiled when they bucked and reared, how she laughed when the exuberant ones farted and kicked.

Rota opened her arms wide, and a massive, bay Belgian stallion trotted over to her, stopping short of headbutting her chest. Instead, he pressed his head into her, leaning so hard that he almost pushed her back. He stood there, eyes closed, as Rota scratched behind his ears and down the crest of his thick neck.

Bryn's heart lurched in her chest, the longing harsh and bitter.

These were Rota's babies, her loves, and the differences between how the horde viewed their horses and how Rota treated hers struck Bryn again. The question was: Had Rota's husbandry made a difference? If the answer was yes, there would be a difficult struggle ahead to overcome the Valkyrie's inured ways.

Helena came back to Bryn and watched with her.

"What's she doing?" Bryn asked.

The stallion backed away and joined the milling horses. Rota crossed her arms and continued to watch them.

"She's letting them warm up. Waiting for dark."

Ashton whinnied and jumped into the fray with the younger horses, the comparison highlighting the signs of the older horse's age. He was glorious, but his reduced muscle mass and the slight sway to his back made it obvious that he was the senior member of the herd.

Shocked by the number of horses—there were at least two dozen—Bryn looked at Helena. "All of them can fly?"

The girl just smiled.

The sun disappeared; night claimed her turn.

Rota dropped her arms and backed away from the group. She walked to the barn doors at the back of the arena and pushed one door open a few feet. The horses came to a stop then walked to Rota, watching her intently, Ashton in the front.

"Ashton, you know better," Rota said softly.

He stamped a foot.

"You can go out, but no flying."

He bobbed his head, his black mane flying up and down, but he walked forward. He reached Rota and she stroked his neck.

"You know why, my friend. The call is not for you anymore." She ran her hand down his body as she walked to his rear end. She patted it gently. "But you will always go first. You will always be their leader. Trot on, big guy."

Bryn struggled to hold back the moisture forming in her eyes. *Not tears, they're not tears. It's the dust.*

Ashton took a deep breath as if resigned to his fate and trotted out of the arena. Rota reached for the other door.

"Come on, we need to hurry now," Helena said.

The pair hustled down the walkway and to the steep stairs in the corner of the arena. Helena ran up the steps, Bryn behind her, until they reached a small door. Helena opened it and crawled inside. Bryn joined her and found she could stand.

Unlike most cupolas that were used for ventilation, this one had tall windows taking up most of each wall, giving the viewer an unobstructed view. Bryn touched the latch on one window.

"The top half of the window opens," Helena said.

"Perfect sniper nest," Bryn muttered under her breath, checking out the 360-degree view.

"That's what I thought!" Helena said, bouncing on her toes. "But that's not the coolest part."

She unlocked the window, pushed the top half open, then climbed out, ending up on the metal roof.

Bryn climbed out after her and trotted slowly along the narrow edge until she joined the girl at the end of the roof, the star-filled sky and full moon yawning above. She shivered, not from the chill, but from an excitement she hadn't known for years. If Rota wasn't lying...

"Sit," Helena said simply, her eyes wide and bright.

Bryn settled next to the girl, her hands fisted, her heart pounding.

Please...

"Fly!" Rota bellowed from below them.

Horses thundered out of the arena, disappearing into the dark. Bryn's fingernails pressed against her palm; she leaned forward as if that would help the horses lift off.

Moonlight hit the huge wings of the first horse, the cool white of the lunar light outlining the feathers and the straining muscles of the sorrel horse fighting to rise into the night.

Bryn gasped then stopped breathing. She leaned farther forward, her toes clenched, her muscles tight as she willed the horse to keep flying until it leveled off and soared. Bryn finally took another breath, only to have it stolen when she saw the mass of horses, every single one that had been in the arena save Ashton, rising to meet their stable mate in the sky.

The moment the last horse joined them, the group took off, rising higher, going faster. They darted and swooped, climbed straight up then fell back, then rose high again only to tuck their wings and their front legs, their necks extended as they rocketed toward the ground, pulling up at the last minute to race past Bryn and Helena, just a few feet above their heads.

Bryn covered her mouth with both hands and laughed as her tears fell. They were playing. They weren't flying as part of a job; these horses were filled with joy for the love of leaving the bonds of earth that so few other horses had ever known.

"It's the most beautiful sight," Helena said softly.

"She did it," Bryn said through her tears.

She swiped them off her face, but they were quickly replaced by fresh ones.

"Yes, I did," Rota said, standing a few feet away.

Bryn and Helena jerked at the same time, followed immediately by a cringe. *Busted. Again.*

"Rota," Helena started to say as she stood.

Rota held up a hand to stop the girl. "I expected better from you. At least some respect for my wishes."

"But—"

"Go inside," Rota said quietly, her disappointment more devastating than her anger would have been.

Bryn watched Helena slump and trudge back to the cupola. No doubt Rota was livid, but Bryn's need to know more chewed up her self-preserving apology. "How?"

Rota turned her attention back to Bryn. She crossed her arms, an all-too-familiar scowl forming on her face. "I've already told you the how, but you won't hear me."

"Don't you see? That's why you must come back to the horde, and with your horses. If you're right…"

"I am," Rota fired back with a roll of her eyes.

"Then only you can prove to them that Odin is the way they'll survive, that they'll fly again. You know how they are; my words aren't going to be enough."

"Why did you pray to Odin earlier?" Rota asked.

"I don't know what you're talking about," Bryn said, forcing down the instinct to clutch the relic under her shirt.

"In the truck. I saw you so don't deny it."

"Why do you care?"

"I don't care so much as I wonder why you would pray to a god whom you've abandoned. Seems hypocritical to me."

Bryn dropped her hands into her lap and watched the horses play above her. "He abandoned us. It was a reflex, a remnant of the elders' stories."

"As long as the Valkyrie cling to that notion, they won't fly. If you can't convince them to recommit to Odin, you will never become a horsemaster because there'll be no horses. You will never save them."

"So, you won't lift a finger," Bryn said, her voice harsh, cracking.

"A finger? I've given you the answer, more than once now. I'll not do more than that; I'll not risk everything I've built here or the safety of the Aries family to return to the people who should have known better than to turn their backs on their god or the family they took an oath to protect."

Rota turned to the cupola.

"He's never answered me," Bryn said. "Odin."

Rota stopped. "Faith is believing even when you don't get an answer. An oath is to be honored even when there's no one there to witness it, or any benefit to be derived from it."

"Damn it," Bryn said, slicing the air with the edge of her hand. "Those are platitudes, and they don't change anything."

"Then the horde is as good as dead."

Rota walked back to the cupola.

"Hey! What about the horses?" Bryn asked.

"They'll be fine. They know their way home." Rota turned her head to nail Bryn with a look of pity mixed with aggravation. "Do you?"

16

Bryn watched the horses until they flew deeper into the mountains and she lost sight of them. She heaved a sigh and made her way back to the house, exhausted by the emotional impact of the experience, and frustrated with herself for not demanding to fly one of them.

She'd been too blown away to do anything but stare, jaw dropped.

Rota left the arena roof long before she did, so Bryn went to the kitchen alone and dug around in the fridge until she found the makings of a killer sandwich. Add in soda and chips and she was set.

Then Helena walked in, scuffing her feet as if on a death march, her head and shoulders hung low. Dejected was the only word to describe it.

"You look like you've been beaten with a switch," Bryn said before taking a huge bite of her sandwich.

Helena flopped into a seat at the bar with a gusty sigh and pulled the loaf of bread to her.

Nothing interfered with this teen and her appetite.

"Almost as bad," Helena said. "I've been getting the 'look' from Nan off and on since we got back. She's really good at working the guilt trip."

"Nan? Is she your grandmother?"

"Nanny. We call her Nan because she's as old as a grandmother and twice as mean."

Bryn chewed for a minute then swallowed. "Why do you keep her around?"

"Because, despite hating the haranguing—"

"Whew, that's a five-dollar word," Bryn teased.

That comment got the flash of a grin from Helena, but her hangdog expression pushed the mirth out and away. "But apt. Despite the words and looks, I know she's right. I way overstepped."

She slathered mustard on the bread slices then picked and pulled from the other ingredients, creating a leaning pile of food that would rival the Pisa tower. Bryn stopped eating for a moment, waiting to see how the girl would be able to take a bite. Not even a snake could unhinge its jaw enough…

Helena climbed onto the seat of her barstool, placed both hands on the top slice of bread, then grunted as she smooshed the sandwich into a manageable size. She settled back in her chair, picked up her sandwich then looked at Bryn's open-mouth stare. "What?"

Bryn blinked and turned her attention back to her food. "Nothing."

The two ate in silence until their sandwiches were gone. Then they dug into the chips, washing down the salty food with their sodas. As one they sat back in their chairs and sighed, rubbing their bellies.

"How soon will your parents get back?"

Helena winced. "A few days."

"That's cutting their trip short?"

Helena sighed and played with her plate. "They were supposed to be gone all summer."

Bryn snorted. "What other kinds of mischief were you planning to get into? Parties, boys?"

Helena pushed her plate away with a flick of her finger and sat up straight. She nailed Bryn with a glare. "I don't find either of those interesting."

"I'll agree on the parties, but boys," Bryn said with a grin. "They have their uses."

"Maybe men do, but not boys my age. I find them tedious and slaves to their hormones. No, I wanted to explore our house even further. Read the books we found, try to understand who and what I am and where I come from. My parents won't tell me, so I had planned to educate myself."

"And now that's blown."

Helena nodded. "The horses too. I now realize that's the greater punishment."

As if on cue, Ashton strolled in and headed for them.

"I don't think I'm ever going to get used to having a horse in the house," Bryn muttered.

Helena got up and went to the fridge. She pulled out a plastic tub, grabbed a dish towel, and returned to her seat. Popping open the lid she took out a piece of watermelon. "The Bedouins shared their tents with their horses. It was a common practice. What about the Valkyrie? I take it you don't let your horses in your homes now, but was there ever a time?"

Ashton rested his head on her shoulder and delicately took the piece from her fingers and munched, his eyes half closed, slobber forming in the corners of his mouth.

Bryn watched the pair: Ashton chewing and drooling, and Helena crooning nonsense to him.

"He's so much better than a boy," Helena said.

Bryn couldn't disagree. "Yes, there was a time that the horde shared everything with their horses. They had to have a strong bond so the horses would answer their call, fly for them."

"What's changed?"

"Odin abandoned us. That's when it all fell apart."

"Because people stopped praying to him, believing in him."

"Yes."

"Seems to me that you and the horde abandoned him right back. I mean, yeah, he fell to Hades, but that was no reason to stop believing in him. Maybe the horses are afraid that you'll do the same to them."

"Kid, I can't imagine the horses being so self-aware that they'd be able to come to that conclusion."

"That seems presumptuous. How would you know what they can and do conclude? Ashton has been through a lot in his years. He was a dressage horse, yet Rota found him at a horse auction, probably destined to be slaughtered for meat. What kind of life had he had? Why would such a highly trained horse be abandoned to slaughter? What did he see, what did he experience, what does he think about what happened over the years? I don't know. No one knows for sure. But I do know that because of Rota he was given a second chance and she believed in Ashton so much that he found his wings. He flew because Rota told him he could."

Helena sighed. "We humans—and I'm lumping the Valkyrie and all the other paranorms with us—shouldn't assume we know so much. It's arrogant and wrong and makes us lesser for it." She offered Bryn the last piece of the sticky fruit. "Want to give him some? He'll love you forever."

Bryn shrugged one shoulder. "Why would I care about him loving me? I won't be here long enough to matter."

Helena stared at her then shook her head, holding out the last piece to his questing lips. "Wow. You didn't hear a word I said."

The watermelon gone, Ashton backed up a few steps then walked down the hall to his bedroom, Bryn presumed. She'd never get used to that either. A horse having his own bedroom...in a house.

Helena stood, took her plate to the sink, rinsed it, and put it in the dishwasher. Still silent, she put away the fixings for the sandwich and threw away the empty chip bag. "On that note, I'm going to bed."

Bryn didn't watch the girl cross the great room, but she cleared her throat before Helena left it. "About the man we saw?"

"Yes," Helena said, not quite able to disguise the excitement in her voice.

"Two words. Black Zodiac."

"What does that mean?"

Bryn looked over one shoulder and shrugged. "Look it up."

"You and me, I thought we were a team. Then you know something huge and don't spill?" Helena's face turned red, and she clenched her fists. "Argh!"

When Bryn remained silent, Helena whirled away and stomped down the hall, muttering under her breath.

Bryn waited until she heard Helena's footsteps fade away before bussing her plate. She washed her hands and studied the hall Helena had used, wondering why she'd said anything at all. She shouldn't have bothered. No, that wasn't true, she wanted Helena to understand what they'd seen and how dangerous it was. Maybe to protect her, maybe to share the knowledge with someone, maybe to reward the girl's courage and curiosity, maybe a combination of all three. Now that she had a start, Bryn had no doubt the intelligent, tenacious girl would figure it out.

Or maybe she hoped to use Helena as a wedge against Rota. She still needed to see if Rota's horses would fly for a Valkyrie, specifically her, without renewing the oath to Odin, because the likelihood of the horde doing that was nil. If she *could* fly one herself, then there'd be hope for her people.

Bryn leaned a hip against the kitchen counter.

No matter the reason for telling Helena about the Black Zodiac, the result was what mattered. The fact that the Black Zodiac existed at all was bad enough; that at least one of them was on ice instead of six feet under was unconscionable if the author of the book was to be believed. How many more were frozen in time? All twelve? Did the other eleven royal houses have their own Black Zodiac on ice?

If Rota banished her from the ranch, someone, namely Helena, needed to understand the danger frozen under her home, if for no other reason than to keep the girl from meddling with the Black Zodiac and getting hurt, or worse, waking the evil.

If Rota did banish her from the ranch, Bryn would give the book to Helena so she could learn the full truth and what it meant.

Bryn pushed off the counter. She had started down the hall to Ashton's bedroom when she heard the clatter of hooves outside the back doors. Curious, she returned to the great room then came to a stop when she saw a long, tall, chestnut horse standing on the patio, looking inside. Its great, red-with-white-tipped wings were folded against its back, the white mark in the middle of its forehead the shape of a pork chop, the three white socks giving him a flash that was belied by his cocked head and pursed lips.

"Well, aren't you handsome?"

The horse cocked his head the other direction and stuck out his tongue.

"And a goofball."

Bryn reached the side door and opened it, easing outside so she didn't spook him. The solid-boned horse bobbed his head and snorted when she approached, but he didn't leave.

"I have missed being around horses," she said, her voice a croon. "Will you let me touch you?"

She held out a hand, her palm up to let him sniff it. His nostrils flared and his breath came out in jets in time with the back and forth flicking of his ears, but he held still when she cupped her palm and touched his mouth.

"I don't have a treat for you. Maybe a scratch?"

She eased closer and raised her hand to his neck, pressing her palm against the smooth, soft coat. Muscle quivered under her hand; he blew more air and took in her scent.

"That's right. Take my measure."

She raised her free hand and, starting at the top of his neck, lightly scratched at the base of his red mane. The horse grunted softly and, cocking his head again, pressed his neck into her nails, the signal he wanted more.

"Like that, do you?" Encouraged by his enthusiasm, she got to work scratching her way down his elegant neck. Reaching the top of his withers, she ran her hands down his long back. "You must be an American Saddlebred."

His huge wings pressed against her belly; the feel of them, their presence, gave her goosebumps. "We're friends now, right? Enough to let me touch your wings?"

He shook his head, making his mane dance, but he didn't move away from her. It wasn't the same as touching them with her hands, but that was not a physical contact a Valkyrie horse accepted easily. Like their mundane brethren, most of the horde's horses had touchy spots: some didn't like their feet lifted, some didn't like anyone near their rear end. Wings were another matter, as if the horses understood the power of them and how vulnerable their wings could be.

Every Valkyrie horse Bryn knew was particular about whom they allowed to touch them.

She stood next to his shoulder and studied the thick, heavy, feather- and sinew- and skin-covered bone tying into the withers and shoulders. How the sheer mass of the wings could disappear completely was magic she didn't understand. But she did understand that this great miracle existed and had accepted her.

Bryn gently laid her hand on the front of the wing and closed her eyes, the horse's heat warming her palm. She explored the wing, using her fingertips to run down the feathers, awed by the fragility of the individual, the power of the whole. Just like the horde.

The horse suddenly turned from her and walked away from the house to an open spot in the yard. He looked at the sky, his body quivering when the moonlight painted the horses still flying.

His wings opened wide.

Bryn's hands shook and she walked quickly to the horse, near breathless from the call that fed every Valkyrie's soul, that bond Odin had bestowed on the horde, the need so deeply nourishing for both horse and rider that they couldn't survive, weren't surviving, without it.

She grasped his red mane, threw her right leg over his back, and pulled herself up. Settling in place, her legs snugged up to the underside of his wings, she squeezed him with her knees.

The horse moved forward at a walk then broke into a trot, his hooves making a soft thumping noise in the grass.

Bryn filled her hands with his mane. "I am a Valkyrie! You must fly—"

His right wing slammed into her side.

Despite her handhold, despite her years of riding and the vice-grip thighs she'd earned because of them, she flew off the horse's back and landed hard several yards away.

The horse came to a stop, opened his mouth, and gnashed his teeth at her. Chastisement given, he wheeled away and took off at a run, lifting off the ground to fly to the others.

Bryn lay in the grass for a long moment, not sure if she could rise, definitely sure the horse hit harder than any Valkyrie ever could. Hell, harder than any semi-truck could, she was absolutely sure.

The relic around her neck slid out from under her shirt. She took it in her hand—at least she could move one arm—gripped it tight, and recited the old prayers to Odin for only the second time since she was a child, too lost in the heartbreak of being torn away from the connection between Valkyrie and horse to feel her tears.

"Please, Allfather. Forgive me for failing you, now and all the years past. I was wrong."

17

Bryn was in the middle of a grand dream that she and the horde were flying in the clouds, wearing their battle armor, the air blowing her hair back and chilling her to the bone. Bracing, some would say. She said it was fucking cold.

The world shifted underneath her. She hit the ground and rolled.

Scrambling to her feet, she crouched, her fists raised, ready to defend herself from the attack even though she had to squint against the blasted sunlight streaming into the room to see her attacker.

Rota stood on the opposite side of the bed, her arms crossed, her expression hard, unforgiving. "No one gets to be a freeloader around here. You eat my food, sleep under my roof, you work. Got that?"

Bryn blinked, trying to figure out what had happened.

The blanket and sheets were a mess. Even the fitted sheet had popped off the mattress. That was her clue.

"You flipped me out of bed?"

Rota walked to the door, speaking without looking back. "Breakfast in five. Get dressed for barn work. And I do mean work."

Ashton snorted.

"You enjoyed that, didn't you?" Bryn asked, straightening, her hands going to the small of her back to rub the knots already forming in the muscle.

He bobbed his head as if agreeing, then slowly collapsed on his side with a groan, punctuated by an impressive fart, like a deflating balloon.

"Yeah, yeah," Bryn said under her breath.

Grabbing her rattiest clothes, she dressed and hustled to the kitchen, finger-combing her nest of hair then pulling it into a ponytail as she went. The bar was filled with platters of eggs and bacon and pancakes; the dining table was filled with the Aries children, the nanny and Rota, all waiting impatiently, if the squirming and frowns were an indicator of their mood.

"Finally!" one of the twins yelled, jumping out of his chair.

The boys climbed onto barstools and loaded their plates with food. Then, as one, and very creepily, they swiveled their heads to the nanny.

"Yes, yes, I know. Good boys for not trying to carry the plates yourselves," the nanny said.

Helena rose from her seat and helped nanny with the plates, the two getting the twins settled before Helena joined Bryn at the bar.

"Have a good night's sleep?" Helena asked, loading her plate even higher than the twins did.

"Good enough."

Helena reached out a hand and gently punched Bryn's right upper arm.

Bryn flinched; the pain from the horse's blow was still really ouchy.

"Oh, are you hurt?" Helena asked, the innocent tone offset by the glint in her eyes.

There were two ways to deal with this: deny all or admit the truth. Bryn didn't like either option, but the girl had obviously witnessed her failure last night. "You saw."

Helena glanced back at Rota. "We both saw you with Rusty."

"So, that's why I got the reception from her this morning."

Helena leaned close. "I think Rota feels sorry for you. I know I do. Those wings can pack a punch."

She returned to the dining table and sat between the twins, stopping the closest one from hurling a syrup-soaked pancake at the wall of glass to see if it would stick.

Bryn's face flushed hot; no doubt her skin was bright red. Her humiliation was beyond complete. It was bad enough she had witnesses to the horse's rejection of her; it was far worse that they'd seen her in the dirt, broken and crying.

She filled her plate and took a seat at the table, expecting Rota to say something about last night and shove her deeper into the depths of her humiliation.

Instead, Rota rose, filled a plate, and returned to the table, silent. Only when she had settled did she bow her head and say, "Hail Allfather, witness this."

Bryn automatically pulled the relic out from under her shirt, gripping the metal tight. "Hail Allfather, witness this."

She glanced at Rota. The woman nodded once, her lips pressed tightly together, then dug into her food.

Whatever Rota thought about last night's debacle, she wasn't planning on sharing it. Nor was she going to crow about it. It was a comfort to Bryn's ego, but a scant one. She dropped her head and forced herself to eat everything. She had no doubt Rota planned to work her to exhaustion or make every effort to that end.

But years of cleaning stables, working the horses, using a scythe to cut down the tallest grasses instead of a mower had kept Bryn and the rest of the Valkyrie in fine shape, at least until recently. It would take more than a hard day's work to fell her.

Meal done and dishes washed and put away, Rota grunted at Helena and Bryn. "Chores."

Nan gathered the twins. "Time for your lessons."

"But we want to play with the horses."

"Not until your work is done and Rota has given her permission."

The boys turned to Rota, their eyes wide, their grins wider.

"When your lessons are done to Nan's satisfaction, I'll show you the new pair of ponies I got."

"Yay!" the boys yelled before running to their room.

"You are far too indulgent with them," the nanny said.

Rota winked at the woman. "But they won't give you a bit of trouble now, will they?"

Nan *humphed* and walked away. "We're starting with math today," she called out. "Aww," the twins complained.

Rota waited a beat then headed for the barn. "Let's go."

Helena trotted ahead of Rota, reaching the barn before the two women did. She pulled on a pair of leather work gloves, set a shovel and rake into a wheelbarrow, and wheeled it away.

Rota pointed at the shelf. "New leather gloves are there. I want you to start in the stall opposite from Helena. Pick the manure, scoop out urine-soaked bedding, and add fresh, wood chips or straw, depending on what's already in each stall." Rota started walking away. "Be glad this isn't stripping day."

Bryn gathered her equipment and trotted down to the stall Rota had pointed out. She entered it and was surprised to find mats on the floor and only a small pile of shavings in one corner.

"Don't all the horses get a full measure of shavings? And why are there mats on the ground instead of hardpack?" Bryn asked.

Helena poked her head out of the stall door. "Every horse is given what they prefer. Some like a lot of bedding, others just their mats and a little bedding to go to the bathroom on. When you have that kind, strip it all out and put fresh in the exact same spot. Don't deviate from what you find in a stall; the horses are very particular about what they want, and very militant if they don't get it."

"Okay," Bryn said. "Where are the horses?"

"They put themselves in the pastures after they fly at night. Rota will call them in when their stalls are clean and their food ready."

"Seems like a lot of work, more than the horde does."

Helena laughed. "Oh, there's no doubt these horses are spoiled rotten, but Rota swears it's made a difference."

"In what?" Bryn asked, quickly filling her wheelbarrow.

She set her shovel against the stall door.

Helena did the same. She jutted her chin toward the open door and walked off with the soiled bedding. "In whether they fly or not."

Bryn followed the girl to a steep ramp that ended at the back of a dump truck.

Helena emptied the wheelbarrow and backed down. "Let's see who gets to the end of the row first."

Bryn dumped the bedding and the two ran to their next stalls. They worked in silence, the rhythm and effort soothing Bryn, the sweat and smells familiar. This was what she had grown up doing, the day-to-day chores required to care for their horses. Clean the stalls, feed the horses, groom them, turn them out in the pastures to graze and play and sleep in the warm sun.

To Bryn's surprise, Helena not only finished first, she raced ahead to the next aisle, laughing at Bryn's dropped jaw.

"Oh, it's on."

They worked steadily. The only sounds were the clop of hooves in the hardpack aisles as Rota brought the horses to their stalls to eat and rest.

Helena was sitting on a bale of hay drinking a soda when Bryn finished her last stall.

The girl patted the large bale then tossed Bryn a bottle. "Time for a break."

Bryn rolled her shoulders and joined Helena. "You're damn fast."

Helena took a drink. "Not so bad yourself." She swiveled on the bale to face Bryn. "So, if the Valkyrie, except for Rota, don't believe in Odin anymore, why do you have that relic around your neck?"

Before Bryn could answer, Rota appeared with the chestnut gelding who'd schooled Bryn the night before. Rusty. She led him to a stall, removed his halter, then shut the door. She wiped the sweat off her brow and held out a hand.

A soda bottle flew and Rota caught it without looking. She walked to the bale and jerked a thumb. "Scoot over."

Bryn made room for the woman and the three leaned against the wall, drinking their sodas in silence.

"Good question, Helena," Rota finally said.

The woman and the girl turned their heads and stared at Bryn.

She choked on her soda and lowered the bottle, pounding her chest with a closed fist to stop the coughing. "At this point, the relic is just a reminder of who we were. Mine was given to me by my mother and she got it from her mother and so on. It also defines which family line we came from."

"A reminder of who you were before you forsook your oath to Odin," Rota said. "Our very existence is owed to him. Are you saying that wearing a piece of his sword is nothing more than a tradition now?"

"Yes, tradition."

"Huh," Rota said with a grunt.

The three fell silent again.

"What now?" Bryn finally asked, the quiet making her twitch.

"School the youngsters, the ones not flying yet, while the horses who do get some sleep."

Bryn smiled. "Can't wait."

Rota slowly turned her head to Bryn. "You're not done cleaning stalls."

"The barn is done."

Rota looked away and took a long drink. "Not all of them." Soda finished, she rose. "Come."

Bryn glared at the woman's back. "What?"

"You'll see," Helena said.

Bryn gave her empty bottle to the girl and trotted after Rota. They walked out the back of the barn and around the corner. Bryn saw two smaller barns, built several yards apart with a tall hedge and heavy fencing separating them.

Rota pointed to the closest barn. "The stallions too fractious to be around the other horses." She pointed to a barn beyond it. "The broodmare barn."

"You have any foals right now?"

Rota smiled, the expression soft and filled with joy. "Yes, we do."

They walked together until they reached the last barn. A single aisle split the barn in two, but the barn was taller and the aisle wider than the standard twelve-foot width.

"I like to give the mares and babies plenty of room to pass the stalls without upsetting the other mares," Rota said. "If I have a mare that's particularly witchy and protective, each stall has an exterior run and gate."

Bryn went to the first stall and gawked at the size. "These are amazing."

"Yeah, they are." Rota opened a door and turned on the light. "In here we have all the equipment and supplies the vet might need for an emergency. And they're on call 24/7."

"Damn, you could do surgery with all this stuff," Bryn said, her voice a whisper.

"The horde still practicing the old ways when it comes to foaling?"

"Yes."

"Still losing some newborns?"

Bryn narrowed her eyes. "Were they when you deserted the horde?"

Rota studied her for a moment as if trying to decide whether to get angry at the dig or let it go. She shrugged. "Yes, but not here."

"Not once?"

"Not once."

Rota waved at Bryn to follow. She stopped at a stall with a top and bottom door, both closed. "This mare just had her baby a few days ago and she's a first timer. Watch her closely; she's protective."

Rota opened the top half of the door and swung it all the way to the wall, latching it. She remained several steps back and waited.

A snort sounded in the far corner, the rustling of straw bedding the only warning of the mare's approach. A head charged out of the shadows and stopped at the door, the golden coat glistening in the light, the near-white mane and forelock swaying as she threw her head, her ears pinned and her teeth gnashing. A gorgeous Palomino making her warning very clear.

Rota pulled a small baggie out of a pocket and handed it to Bryn. "You'll have to find a way to make friends so you can get inside the stall without getting hurt."

Bryn held up the bag. "Candy?"

"Skittles. She adores them and they're the only way to keep your hide intact."

"What's her name?"

"Hel." Rota snorted, her grin lopsided as she backed away. "Good luck."

"Rota," Bryn called out.

The former horsemaster looked back.

Bryn's words stuck in her throat. The question "why" hung there, needing to be spoken, yet her pride, of which she was said to have more than her fair share, kept the mention of last night from escaping. From the words being released, never to be taken back. From admitting her failure.

Rota's hard, implacable expression, the one she wore like armor, softened just a hair. Barely enough to be noticeable, but it was there. She paused a beat. "Because when you were at your lowest, you called to the Allfather for solace and forgiveness."

Rota turned away and quickly left the barn, as if chased away by the kindness.

Bryn watched her back until Rota disappeared inside the main barn. She glanced down at the Skittles. "Well, damn." She heaved a sigh, squared her shoulders, and gave Hel a long look. "That was unexpected."

The mare tossed her head and placed herself between the door and her foal, making her wishes known. *Stay away from my baby.*

Skittles or not, Hel wasn't going to make this easy.

"Time for some ingenuity."

Pocketing the bag of candy, Bryn walked out of the barn and turned right, heading for the back of the stall and the run attached to it.

Other mares and foals had been released, the mares giving Bryn the stink-eye as she passed them, counting out the stalls until she reached the one holding Hel.

The run had a gate at the opposite end from the stall, which could make it tricky if Hel and her baby raced out and blocked her escape. The wood fence was tall but the rails were placed just far enough apart to make the fence a ladder of sorts. That, plus the extra space between the runs to prevent fighting, gave her an escape route in case she couldn't reach the gate.

That Rota hadn't mentioned this option was insulting. Did she really think Bryn was so stupid she couldn't figure out this was a better way to release the mare and foal than going through the stall?

She opened the gate, slipped inside, then latched it, making sure it was secure. She didn't want the mare and foal to get loose. The mares on either side of the run stopped eating their hay and stood facing her.

As if waiting for the show.

Her hackles raised, an itch worked its way down her spine, but she shrugged it off. She'd handled horses since she was old enough to walk, her chubby hands grasping the lead rope of some more dangerous than Hel.

She walked to the stall and studied the Dutch door. She could open the top half to give Hel warning that she was there, or she could open top and bottom as one to give her a head start to the gate. Or over the fence if it came to that.

She unbolted both doors, took a deep breath, and opened them together. Silence from the stall. Not a squeal or a snort.

Okay then.

Bryn started for the back, hugging the fence and keeping her eyes on the open stall, just in case. She was within a few feet of the gate, almost close enough to touch it, when Hel charged out of the stall and rushed past her.

The mare pushed her body between Bryn and the gate, her neck low, her ears pinned.

Bryn put her feet in reverse. She pulled the Skittles out of her pocket and shook the bag but that seemed to piss off the mare. "Come on now, I know you love the candy. Rota told me so."

Bryn kept backing up.

The mare started forward, one slow step at a time. Bryn opened the bag and gently tossed Skittles on the ground, hoping to distract her.

And it would have worked if the foal hadn't taken that moment to cry out, with Bryn between the baby and its very unhappy mama.

"Crap me."

Bryn threw the bag through the fence and reached for the highest board. She had turned away from the mare and lifted a leg to seat a toe when Hel's wings erupted from her body.

Wide with pearlescent, white feathers, the wings were stunning, unlike anything Bryn had seen or heard of in the horde's stories. They glowed in the sun, mesmerizing, as if having a life of their own, until Hel whirled and one of the wings slapped Bryn against the barn.

She hit the wall hard and slid to the ground, stars and black spots filling her vision field until all she could see was the outline of the approaching mare.

Bryn tried to roll over—she wanted to crawl into the stall before Hel stomped her—but the foal's head appeared in the sunlight, his body still in shadow. He stayed there, blocking Bryn's chance at escape.

Humiliation coursed through her. First, she was rejected by a horse last night, and now she was about to be stomped by another. Where had her savvy gone? What had happened to her skill with the horses? Why had she thought she could be a horsemaster when she couldn't even manage to turn a horse out?

The relic weighed heavy on her chest, warmed by her skin. She pulled it out and gripped it tight, wanting to recite a prayer to Odin but still too stunned to recall the words. She sagged and waited; even adrenaline couldn't drive her to fight...or run.

The foal stepped out fully into the sunlight and walked up to her, blowing air out of his nostrils, his body tense in case he needed to run. He stopped next to her and dropped his nose to the relic, lipping it for a second, tugging on the leather thong.

"Like that, do you?"

Bryn reached up with her left hand and offered it to the foal. He dropped the relic and sniffed then pushed his nose into her palm. "You are a handsome one."

He had a white-blond mane and tail, but his rough foal coat was several shades darker than his mother's medium gold. If the color of his adult coat remained the same, it would be a stunning dark gold. An uncommon color for a Palomino.

Hel stopped walking toward her.

Bryn glanced at the mare and wondered why she hadn't gone berserk at the interaction between Bryn and the foal. Instead, Hel dropped her head and nuzzled the ground until she found a Skittle. She cupped it with her lips, pulled it into her mouth, and started chewing, Bryn forgotten for the pleasure of the sweet-tart treat.

"Oh, now you want the candy."

The foal walked over to Hel and butted her flank before turning his head to nurse.

Bryn sagged for a moment while she took inventory of the aches making themselves painfully known. Of all the scenarios she'd imagined for this trip, being beat to shit multiple times, and shot, hadn't been on the list of possibilities.

Considering the mare could go on the offensive at any moment, Bryn needed to make a move while Hel was preoccupied. She rolled onto her hands and knees and crawled into the stall, then pulled the door closed and latched it.

"Wow, you look awful," Helena said from the front door. "Need the first aid kit?"

She held up a huge, plastic box with a red cross on it.

Sagging again, Bryn let out a huge breath of relief and gripped the relic, her limbs weak. "Shut up, kid."

19

"Do can do, Valkyrie," Helena said. "I need you up and functioning so we can clean this barn. Rota's getting the stallion barn done."

Bryn groaned and pulled herself onto her feet. "We'll get it done, but why are you bouncing on your toes?" *And giving me a headache in the process.*

Helena promptly stopped the bouncing and grinned. "Can't say, Rota's orders, but it's good." She waved at Bryn. "Come on."

Bryn walked along the stall, using her hands to help her balance until she steadied up a bit. Reaching the door, she exited in time to see Helena stow the first aid kit in a storeroom then pull out a wheelbarrow and shovel and stall fork for picking manure.

"Take this one," the girl said. "You do one side and I'll do the other, just like before."

Bryn headed to the first stall. She had started cleaning when a sound in the distance caught her attention. She paused and cocked her head but didn't hear anything.

"I must have knocked my head harder than I thought," she muttered.

She walked to the stall entrance to dump the forkful of manure into the wheelbarrow and heard the distinct crack of gunfire in the distance. She dumped the fork and ran outside, searching for the source.

Horses screamed from far in the huge pasture, most running, but two limping hard as they tried to keep up. Another *crack* sounded; a third horse screamed and began limping before it staggered and fell to the ground.

A wave of hot, sick recognition hit Bryn in the chest. She sucked in a deep breath. "Helena!"

The girl looked out of the stall she was cleaning, pulling earbuds out. "What's up?"

"Get the horses in their stalls! Close them up tight then close the barn and bar the doors! Stay inside and do not come out for anyone but me or Rota!"

The broodmares squealed and kicked, their agitation rising with every second. "What's happening?"

Bryn pointed at the girl and scowled. "Do as I say, now, before the mares panic and hurt their foals. Do it!"

Helena threw her shovel in the barrow and closed the stall door before running to the back and opening that door. The mare and foal ran inside, blowing and stamping, terrified.

Another *crack*. Another scream.

Bryn took off at a dead run for the stallion barn. "Rota!"

Rota erupted out of the barn, bareback on a huge, bay Belgian stallion, controlling him with her legs and the thin, leather strap resting at the base of his massive neck. In her right hand two large compound bows and a quiver, the second quiver already strapped across her chest. Next to them, Rota controlled another stallion with the same kind of neck strap, this one almost as tall and solid black—a Warmblood of some kind—his long mane and tail flying as they galloped closer.

Bryn turned her back to the black stallion and started running parallel to him, gaining momentum, tensing her muscles. The timing had to be just so, or *crunch*.

Bryn felt the air push past her before he reached her. She looked back, reached out her left hand, and grabbed the neck strap, while kicking off the ground. She flung her right leg over the back of the stallion and settled into the horse's rhythm.

"Gunshots. Someone's shooting the horses," she yelled at Rota.

Rota's answer was to toss her the quiver then the bow.

"No rifles?" Bryn asked, securing the quiver.

"They aren't trained for the shock of the sound," Rota answered.

A scream echoed out of the arena. Ashton bolted through the open doors and turned, heading straight for the men at a gallop.

"Holy shit," Bryn yelled. "What do we do?"

"You get in the pasture and put yourself between whoever's shooting and the horses. I'm going around to cut Ashton off before he gets himself killed."

The tall pasture fence was fast approaching.

"This guy knows how to jump?"

Rota gave her a pained half-grin. "More than I'd like him to. Point him at it and hang on."

"You know who's doing this?" Bryn yelled as Rota guided her horse away.

"Take a wild guess," Rota shouted.

"Mr. C's sonofabitch family and friends, I'll bet," Bryn said to herself, Rota being too far away to hear her.

The gunfire increased. The horses in the pasture had gotten far enough away that the bullets missed. But there was still one horse down and in range. Bryn had to get between them, so they didn't kill the poor animal.

The stallion snorted and increased his speed, his ears up, his gaze on the fence.

Bryn pulled the bow across her body and leaned into the horse's stride, lacing her fingers in his mane, gripping it tight. She panted through the adrenaline. Damn the fence was tall.

"Make it count!" she called out to the stallion.

His muscles bunched and he collected his stride, anticipating the push off. She judged the distance.

"Now!" she yelled, leaning forward.

He rocketed into the air. Bryn gripped her legs around his barrel and held onto his mane against the forces trying to push her back and unseat her. The stallion cleared the fence with room to spare.

But now for the landing.

He grunted when his front feet sank into the dirt and grass, his back arched

115

first then bowed when his rear legs pulled up, before shooting forward to land. Bryn concentrated on staying on his back as he pushed off with his incredibly strong rear end. They sprang forward and the jump was over.

Bryn sat up and released his mane. "Let's see how much legwork you know."

She pulled the bow off her chest and removed an arrow from her quiver. Using her knees and feet, she steered the stallion in the direction of the grounded horse, pushing him into a gallop that ate up the yards.

They reached the downed horse and circled it once to slow down before stopping in front of it. Bryn jumped off the stallion and placed herself in front of him and the injured horse.

She raised the bow, notched the arrow, noting the slightly larger than normal, blunted tip, then looked for the assholes who'd shoot defenseless animals. Her rage spilled over when she spotted them at the fence line, standing in the beds of their parked trucks.

"Let's see how you like it when you're the target."

Ashton came into her peripheral vision; he'd be on the men any second. They pivoted where they stood; one man raised his rifle and aimed it at the approaching horse, but Ashton pinned his ears and sped up, fury making him fly on the ground.

"You will not harm one hair..."

She pulled the compound bow hard, sighted her target, then raised the bow slightly to account for the arc of the arrow's flight. She took a breath, held it, and released the arrow.

Dirt flew up a few feet in front of her, but she ignored the close shot and waited for the arrow to finish its flight. Then smiled when the man aiming at Ashton fell out of the truck bed.

Immediately she pulled another arrow out of the quiver and found her next target, letting that arrow fly.

Another bullet hit the ground inches from her. It wouldn't be long before they found her, so she moved away from the horses to give the men a new target, one that could fight back and keep their attention.

Her second arrow found its target; the man fell out of his truck bed.

Notch another arrow, aim...

A bullet grazed her outer thigh.

She flinched but kept the bow taut, waiting for the adrenaline to ease so she'd stop shaking, but before she could settle, the Belgian rose into the sky behind the trucks, its four black wings huge and beating hard to fight gravity's pull.

Bryn lowered her bow and gawked, oblivious to her surroundings, her peril, her wound, too enraptured by the Valkyrie warrior and her steed flying in the daylight, preparing to engage the enemy like the horde of old.

20

Rota raised her bow and let two arrows fly at once, both hitting their target.

Bryn dropped her bow and quiver and ran to the injured horse. She searched for the wound and found the mare was shot in the meaty part of her shoulder. Painful, but not as bad as it could have been.

Bryn took off her tee shirt, bunched it up and pressed it to the wound. The mare flinched and raised her head.

"Steady there, don't try to stand. We're going to make this better," she crooned to the horse, stroking her long, elegant neck.

Now would have been a good time for the first aid kit, but she didn't want to leave the mare, and Helena had followed her instructions exactly, so the girl didn't know to bring it.

A heavy thud sounded yards away and Bryn half smiled at the sight of the Belgian's stunning wings as he galloped toward them.

Rota slowed him, jumping off his back before he stopped, the momentum helping her run forward. She slipped onto her knees next to the mare and pushed Bryn out of the way. "How bad is it? Does she need surgery?"

Bryn lay in the grass, too surprised by Rota's shove to get angry. Of course, Rota would do that. The woman was a horsemaster through and through; the horses always came first.

"It's in the meaty part of her shoulder," Bryn said. "She can be sedated right here, and the bullet removed. Some hydrotherapy and antibiotics and she'll be fine." Bryn glanced at the empty truck beds. "Are they dead?"

Rota finished checking the wound and covered it again with Bryn's shirt. "Not dead, but they'll sleep long enough for you to bind them and call the cops. When the sheriff gets here, tell him I'm pressing charges. But before that, send Helena out here with the supplies you mentioned."

"You agree?"

"Yeah, now go."

Bryn rose and dusted off her jeans and her bare skin, the fresh aches making themselves known. She wanted to ride again, to feel a horse under her, but the black stallion had wandered off and she didn't have the energy to catch it. Instead, she started for the gate.

"Valkyrie," Rota said.

Bryn glanced back. Rota's gaze was still on the horse

Rota paused then looked up, her agony for the mare and her appreciation for Bryn's help warring expressions on her face. "Bryn."

"Yeah?"

"Good job," Rota said with a quick nod.

Bryn nodded back and walked away. She wanted to tell Rota, *Thank you for trusting me, thank you for letting me witness the fury and retribution only a Valkyrie can inflict.* She wanted to ask why she couldn't fly the black stallion by Rota's side.

One foot in front of the other, mouth shut, was what she did instead.

* * *

Bryn finished tying up the last man, pleased to see that they'd all suffered abrasions and small cuts when they'd fallen, less pleased that the bastards weren't dead. She'd been right; these were Mr. C's sons and two of their friends, the same foursome who'd scared Helena, given Bryn a helluva beating, and broken into the Aries home.

"Why the hell aren't you still in jail?"

Ashton pranced around the men, terribly pleased with himself despite Bryn's scolding the moment he was in earshot.

Bryn turned on the gelding and planted her fists on her hips. "What the hell were you thinking? Huh? They could have killed you."

Ashton pawed at the ground and shook his head.

She stepped closer. "Don't shake me off, you brat. I get why you did it; you're the boss hog around here." She stalked over to the pile of rifles and picked one up, holding it high. "But this weapon is stronger than you. This weapon can kill you."

Ashton walked up to her, his snorty attitude dissipating with every step. Bryn lowered the rifle then held it out to him. He blew out his nostrils before extending his neck and taking a good, long sniff of the stock. He continued up the rifle to the forestock then the barrel.

"Remember this, Ashton. If you see this, run."

He backed away. The ground vibrated slightly. Bryn turned and saw the horses circling Rota and Helena and the injured horse.

"Go help the horses," she whispered to Ashton. "They're confused and scared, and they need their leader."

He stared at her for a long moment as if weighing his choices, which was nuts, before he turned away and trotted off to the open pasture gate.

Seriously, the horse is a genius.

A groan sounded from behind her.

Bryn walked up to one of Mr. C's sons and squatted next to him. "You really screwed up this time. Shooting innocent horses? You're damn lucky Rota had arrows with anesthetic tips. Me? I would have killed you and buried your body where no one would have found you."

"You fucking bitch," he slurred.

"That's exactly what I am. I'm also going to be the one to take you, your brother, and your friends out if I ever see you here again or if you come near Helena or her brothers. Not Rota, me."

"I'll kill you," he said, shaking as he pushed off the ground.

"You'll try. You'll fail."

She stood and watched him try to rise.

"Then we'll teach Helena a lesson she'll never forget. Make a woman of her," he said, grinning at Bryn. "We own everything and everyone from Aspen to Leadville, so there's nothing you can do to stop us."

The promise in his eyes chilled her. The certainty that he meant every word, and worse, cemented what she needed to do.

She pulled the short dagger from her boot and held it lightly between her thumb and forefinger, waggling it so he wouldn't miss it. With her free hand she lifted his black tee shirt.

He kicked the ground with his heels, trying to escape her. "What the hell?"

Bryn straddled him. "You claim to own everything around here, but I own you."

She grabbed his skinny neck and leaned hard, holding him in place. She made a diagonal cut from his left nipple to the base of his breastbone, right at the start of his white stomach.

He screamed and writhed, but the anesthetic had weakened him.

She pushed harder on his throat until he stilled, his body shaking under her. She flipped the dagger and carved a second diagonal line, connecting them at the base to form a wide vee.

He flinched and squirmed but couldn't break free or was too frightened to try. Some fought until death; others gave up early.

Guess I know which category this boy falls under.

"Please stop."

"Now with the polite?" Bryn grinned. "Not until I'm finished."

She flipped the dagger again then quickly sliced two long, parallel lines from the bottom of the vee, past his belly button, to the waistband of his baggy jeans. She finished with a diagonal cut that bisected the parallel lines.

He whimpered; his skin twitched at the insult.

"Please," he whispered, tears rolling from his eyes to his ears.

Bryn tucked the dagger in her boot and stood, stepping away from the coward. "I've branded you an enemy of the Valkyrie. If another of my kind finds you, they will take you from your worthless, privileged life and you will know hell on earth. Stay away from here, stay away from the entire Aries family, and for Odin's sake, make a real man of yourself. Have I made myself clear?"

He curled into a ball and nailed her with a hate-filled stare, but he nodded.

The crunch of tires on gravel caught Bryn's attention. "Oh, look, the sheriff is here. Have fun in jail."

A car pulled up and a tall mountain climbed out.

"Ira? What are you doing here?" she asked.

"Get her, you great buffoon. Take her down! Now!" the man she'd carved up yelled. He pulled up his bloody shirt. "Look what she did to me."

Ira walked with long strides and took her arm, pulling her away from the men on the ground. He turned her to face him, his back to the others. "What did you do?"

"Me?" she said, her voice strident. "I stopped them from killing the horses. As it is they shot four of them. They're lucky Rota chose to leave them alive. I would have killed them."

Ira's eyebrows met in the middle when he frowned.

She wanted to take a step back from the anger in his expression. *He isn't as mild-mannered as I thought.*

"Are the horses going to be okay?"

"They will be."

Ira stepped closer. "And you?"

Bryn craned her neck back, her knees growing wobbly when she smelled him. What was it about this man that made her want to woman up and do a full-on swoon? She tilted her head one way then the other until her neck popped, and she was able to overcome the impulse.

"Hey, how did you get here so quick?" she asked.

He stepped back. "I, uh, heard the call on the scanner. I was…close by so I wanted to check on you."

She watched a flush start at his neck and work its way up to his hairline. He was a terrible liar, but she didn't have time to drag the truth out of him.

She shrugged. "Uh-huh. No matter. When the sheriff gets here, these bastards are going to jail."

"For a couple hours, maybe, but they'll get bail and be out after that."

The sound of sirens coming up the road caught Ira's attention. He backed away but kept his gaze on Bryn.

"Be careful," he mouthed before turning to the men, his focus solely on them now.

21

"**Y**ou did what?" Rota yelled.

Bryn shrugged. "I carved the Valkyrie symbol for enemy into his skin. Scared the crap out of him, and now the four bastards are headed to jail. I don't think they'll bother you or the Aries family again."

Rota pulled a dining chair out from the table and sank into it. She dropped her head into her hands. "Oh, they won't have to. Mr. C will send more to cause me hell." She raised her head and leveled a hard stare at Bryn. "You've just put all our lives, especially the horses', at great risk."

Confused by Rota's words, a cold sweat swamped Bryn, Rota's fear breaking through her bravado. "He only has two sons; who's he going to send?"

Rota sat back and stared out the wall of glass, a pained expression on her scarred face. "He has fighters all over the state and he knows everything about each one. The man has damn journals of information about every person who fights for him. It's another way to control them."

"Including you?" Bryn asked, finally taking a seat.

"Yes, though he doesn't know what I really am." She drummed the table with her fingers. "Some of the fighters are looking for a payday; some are looking to ease the boredom and stress of their lives. Some are looking for an excuse to spill blood because they love to hurt people and fighting is the only way they can and not end up in prison. Those are the men Mr. C would send, men who have no compunction about killing people, much less the horses."

"Then why did you press charges?" Bryn pressed.

"Because the proof was right there; it couldn't be ignored by the sheriff. But his sons will be out of jail by tonight, if not earlier."

"There's no way they will come back here. Not after what I did," Bryn said, sure that her threat had done the trick.

"The sons probably won't be back—it was a bone-headed move on their part—but you made it personal to Mr. C when you carved the symbol into his son's skin. He would have shrugged off the charges and maybe even ordered his boys not to come out here again. Now, though, Mr. C won't be able to let it stand. You got the better of his flesh and blood...again."

The truth of what her impulse, her arrogance, would bring down on them hit Bryn in the gut. She sat back and struggled to draw a breath, the image of the horse going down from the gunshot fresh in her mind, a jagged stake in her heart. Her petty revenge could cost them dearly. The horses and the people she'd begun to care about, and ultimately the horde—they'd all pay a dear price for her actions.

"How long do you think we have before he moves on us?" she asked, her voice low, the hitch in it too powerful to hide.

Not that Bryn wanted to hide her shame and regret from Rota. Her right to her pride had ended the moment she put knife tip to flesh.

"He'll send them in waves; that's what he does. Frontal assault, day after day until we're no more," Rota said, almost under her breath, her eyes glazed over as if seeing the attack.

"Can you fly the horses out of here? Get them away?"

"I could hide them deep in the mountains, sure, but what about the horses who can't fly, what about the mares and foals? There are too many who'd need to be trailered out."

"But—" Bryn said.

Rota held up a hand. "Mr. C will have all the roads watched. If we try to drive the horses out, they'll run us off the road. A tragic accident would be the pronouncement. Case closed."

"Damn."

"I think we have tonight," Rota continued. "I'm going to fly Helena, her brothers, and Nan out of here, hide them away with every horse who can fly."

Bryn's breath caught in her throat, the thought of flying, finally, gripping her tight. "I'll help."

"By staying here. I can't risk leaving the other horses alone," Rota said.

Bryn slumped in her chair. The woman was right, but by the Allfather, when would she get to fly?

"Then what?"

Rota finally turned her gaze on Bryn, her pallor alarming. "Then I'm going to offer Mr. C something he's wanted for years."

"What's that?"

Rota pushed out of the chair, her palms against the heavy, wooden table as if needing the support.

She took a deep breath. "My life."

* * *

Bryn watched the horses lift off into the dark sky, the squeals of delight from the children almost drowned out by Nan's never-ending screams of "This isn't possible!" Rota had given Bryn a huge list of to-dos, with many still left after an afternoon-worth of work, but every item was necessary to prepare them for an attack.

Even after hours of pestering, Bryn still hadn't gotten Rota to clarify what she meant about Mr. C wanting her life. Obviously, it was bad, but what exactly did she mean?

Ashton stopped next to Bryn and blew softly on her shoulder.

She reached up and cupped his muzzle without looking away from the last view of the horses. "Why didn't you go with them?"

He rested his head on her shoulder.

"You stayed to protect the rest, didn't you?"

Using his head, he pulled her in until her back was against his chest. He held her there as if she were now another member of his herd, another soul to protect.

Bryn stayed caught, her hands on the bridge of his nose, her eyes welling as she let herself release the tension. "I messed up, big time, and I don't know how to fix it."

Ashton dropped his head lower, and she wrapped her arms around him, breathing deep the smell of horse. They stayed that way for several minutes until Bryn released him and stepped away. She swiped at her tears and pulled the checklist out of her back pocket.

"Enough of that, I have work to do. Keep me company?"

Ashton nodded.

Bryn shook her head even as she smiled. "Serious genius." She had started for the door to get the interior work done when a flash of light caught her attention. "Crap."

She ran for the front door and cracked it open.

A car pulled up—slid to a halt if truth be told—stirring up a cloud of dust.

Bryn waited, expecting a group of men to bail out of the car and charge for the door, but only the driver's side door opened. A man tumbled out, falling to his hands and knees.

"Bryn," he called out.

Bryn opened the door wide. "Ira!"

"Help," he said, pushing off the ground but still on his knees. "Please."

Bryn ran to him and gasped at the blood covering his face, the swelling eyes that would soon be shut. She took one of his huge arms and pulled him onto his feet. "What happened? Who did this to you?"

"Where's Rota?" He sagged against Bryn. "I need to talk to her."

"She'll be back tonight, but it'll be a while." She tugged on him, pulling him toward the house. "Let's get you inside."

He followed her, almost docile.

Bryn led him to the dining table and made him sit before she got a good look at his face. The huge man had taken a beating, but when she lifted his hands, they were unbroken, unbruised. He hadn't landed a single blow.

"Holy Odin. Why didn't you fight back?"

"Couldn't," he said simply through cracked, swollen lips.

His whole body shuddered and he sagged into the chair, wincing when he moved.

"Sit tight." Bryn ran into the kitchen, grabbing a pair of towels and two bags of frozen peas. She pressed the wrapped peas against his eyes. "What happened? Why are you here for Rota? Did Mr. C send you?"

How fast can I find a weapon to defend myself if he turns on me?

She glanced around for suitable options.

He took a shallow breath and winced again.

"Where else are you hurt?" He didn't reply so she reached for the buttons of his flannel shirt, undoing them quickly then peeling the shirt off him. "Crap."

His ribs had already turned dark blue and black, the bruises disappearing under the hair on his chest. She examined each rib as gently as she could, but he cried out at almost every touch.

"What? Did they take a bat to you?"

Ira nodded. "They took my mother."

"Mr. C?"

He nodded again, then shook his head. "Not Mr. C himself. His men did it under his orders."

"Why?"

"Because I didn't teach you a lesson when I came here before. Because Mr. C gave me an order and I refused."

"Okay, I want you to sit here while I get some bandages. I need to wrap your ribs so you don't injure something inside you."

"It'll hurt."

"Yes, it'll hurt, but once I'm done it won't hurt as much. Okay?" she asked, touching his forearm to soothe him, and steady herself if she were honest.

He nodded again.

"Then tell me the rest of the story."

128

22

Bryn finished wrapping Ira's ribs, almost as relieved to be done as he was. She'd never heard a man moan so often or so loudly. "Alright, I'm done. Feel better?"

"Some."

"Can you stand? We need to get you horizontal."

They struggled to get him out of the chair; he wobbled a bit and Bryn said a rare prayer to the gods that he didn't go down and take her with him. She'd be crushed by his mass. She guided him to the bedroom Helena had used, happy to see the bed was king-sized.

Ira sat down hard, sweat running down his face and upper body. "I think I'm going to pass out now."

He fell back and that was that. His head landed on the pillows, which was good, but his legs were still off the bed. Not so good.

Bryn dropped her chin to her chest. "So much for the rest of the story."

She couldn't leave him like that, but damn his legs were massive. She tried lifting his right leg by the foot and ankle but her back screamed. *Not happening.*

"Ashton."

He stuck his head in the door.

"I need your help." Grabbing a flat sheet from the closet, she folded it then knotted the ends, creating a closed loop. "This side."

Ashton rounded the bed and stood still while she looped the sheet around Ira's calf. She waved the horse closer and slipped the other end over his head.

"We pull together. Slowly."

Ashton backed up and Bryn pulled until Ira's right leg was on the bed. They repeated the maneuver on his left leg until the man was fully prone.

"You are seriously getting a lifetime supply of watermelon." Bryn wiped the sweat off her brow and eyed Ira's jeans. "Now for the last phase."

She grunted and sweated even more but she managed to pull his jeans off, cringing when she saw the horrid bruises on his legs. It seemed the only thing they'd spared was his genitalia. The man had taken a beating that would have killed any other man; the only thing saving him was his size and thick muscle.

Bryn gently covered him with a blanket then removed the bags of peas from his eyes. He'd have some serious shiners for a few days, but the swelling had already gone down quite a bit; he wouldn't be blinded by it.

She swept a thick lock of hair from his forehead then turned out the light. *Let him sleep. Let his body rest.*

She still had her list to see to, and now she had rage to tamp down and mold so she could use it effectively. But first...

She closed the bedroom door, then startled when a soft, golden light appeared under the door. *Guess the man doesn't like to sleep in the dark.*

She strode to the great room and found a cell phone, dialed the sheriff's office, asked one question, then hung up, fighting the urge to throw the phone against the wall. Just as Rota said, Mr. C's sons and his friends had been bailed out of jail two hours after they'd arrived. No doubt they, or someone else, had been ordered to attack Ira and take his mother, but why? Ira hadn't shown any disloyalty to Mr. C. The man had a kind heart and had even warned her to be careful, but Caldwell's brutal response seemed disproportionate.

She laid the phone down on the kitchen counter. Mr. C was moving fast; Bryn needed to move faster. The broodmares and their foals had been moved into the barn; the stallions who didn't fly had been moved into the arena stalls. All the stalls had been very carefully selected by Rota, much to Bryn's confusion.

The barn and arena doors had been shut, all the windows shuttered. The metal exterior was solid and fireproof. Now Bryn's job was to secure the house itself.

She hustled through the list, shutting down any weak points, until she reached the last item: *How to access Rota's weapons.* She read the instructions.

"Hot damn!"

Bryn ran to Rota's bedroom and dropped to her knees at the end of the bed. She felt around until she found a recessed button and pushed it, the whir of a motor starting immediately. She fell back then scrambled to her feet and watched the end of the huge bed rise slowly.

She grinned when a light came on, illuminating the steps leading into the dark hide. She stepped into the hole and continued down, down, down into the deep basement, where she found a light switch at the base of the steps and flipped it.

A long trail of lights blinked on. This was no small hide, but a very deep, very long, very wide basement. The sheer breadth must encompass the entirety of the three-building structures above her head.

She'd never seen anything like it.

Bryn trotted around the space, never coming close to seeing it all, but not missing the food stores for humans and horses, and water barrels lining the walls. Nor did she miss the stalls built in random places around the basement.

What the hell?

She rubbed her face. Rota had planned for this eventuality from the start. Did she know the humans would cause her problems? Or had the former Valkyrie created this to protect her horses from the horde? She could understand the former, but the latter caused her heart to sink. This had been built for either scenario, which meant Rota had no plans to ever help the horde.

Of all the things Rota could have said or done, this evidence closed the door. Maybe not finally if Bryn could convince Rota otherwise, but it was damning proof that Rota considered the horde a serious threat. One that she had planned and built extensively to counter. The only whisper of hope remaining was that

Rota had allowed Bryn to see the basement. That was a serious act of trust...or desperation. For now, Bryn chose to hope that it was the former.

"Enough. This isn't getting the job done."

She made her way back to the stairs and found four long, tall, metal cabinets against a wall. Opening the cabinet on the far left, Bryn gasped.

Hundreds of lethal-tipped arrows—for killing, not tranquilizing—had been collected into large quivers, while bows of various sizes hung next to them.

"Nice." She opened the next cabinet and reached out to touch the swords and knives, axes and hammers, spears and maces. "Praise the Allfather."

The third cabinet was double-sized; its contents took her breath away. Golden armor, sized for horses, hung there, glittering in the soft light.

As the horde had lost the ability to fly, and been left to fend for themselves for years, the armor had been sold off to feed them. Bryn had only seen a single piece of armor when she was a child; she'd never seen a full set of the priceless protection. She longed to touch them, but reverence stayed her hands.

Stepping back, she eyed the final cabinet. What could possibly be more precious than horse armor? She touched the latch, lifted it, and the doors swung open on their own.

Metal wings made of gold, forged to be worn by the Valkyrie. Bryn couldn't breathe; she couldn't blink. These were myth, legend. Wings hadn't been seen for centuries, not since the gods and goddesses had fallen to Hades, trapped there while the Valkyrie slowly fell apart.

She didn't even try to touch them, afraid they would disappear, shimmer away back into the mists of the past as if they were a mere illusion.

But she remembered the books, the drawings of the oldest of the horde, the art handed down for generations. Drawings of the Valkyrie "flying" in battle. Not that the wings flapped like a bird's, but when fully extended they allowed the Valkyrie to leap from their horses and glide. When the wings were folded, the Valkyrie could pierce the air in a freefall, decimating their target before using the wings to soften their landing.

They were magic and blood and terror rolled into a precious, gold package.

Bryn picked arrows and bows from the first cabinet then slowly closed all the cabinet doors, leaning on the last one for a long moment, collecting her scattered thoughts.

"Bryn!"

"Down here, Rota."

Footsteps rushed down the stairs.

Bryn walked up to the woman and handed her some of the weapons.

"Everyone settled?" she asked, her voice breaking after the revelations of the past few minutes.

"They're safe. Mr. C will never find them. So, you want to share why Ira is here?"

Bryn climbed the stairs in silence. She stopped next to the bed and waited for Rota to join her.

"Did you bother to look at him?" she snapped.

Rota's eyebrows rose high, but she kept her voice soft. "Someone beat the crap out of him."

"With a bat. They took his mother, though he passed out before he could tell me what order Mr. C gave him and why he refused."

"If I were to guess, Mr. C ordered him to come here and kill us."

Bryn left the bedroom and entered the great room. She dropped the bows and arrows on the table and crossed her arms. "Guess his loyalty lies elsewhere."

"With me?" Rota asked, placing her weapons gently on the table. "If it's anyone, it's you. He's sweet on you."

Goosebumps rose and Bryn shivered at the thought. No one had been sweet on her, not ever. Not that she cared; she'd set her eyes on one prize and men had no place in her plans.

"What? Why the hell would you think that? It was you he came to see, you he asked for, not me."

"Ira is well-liked by the fighters, at least most of them. He could have gone to one of them for help, but instead he comes here? I don't know why he'd do that other than you were here. Otherwise, I'd have to wonder if we're being set up. If he's being used as a plant inside my place."

"Screw that. You didn't see his injuries. No one takes that kind of punishment to be a plant."

"Okay, Bryn. What do you suggest we do about him? I vote to slit his throat and continue prepping for what's coming."

Bryn shifted her body and pulled a long dagger out of her boot in the span of a breath. She crouched, blocking Rota from the bedroom door leading to Ira. "I'll kill you before you even get inside the bedroom."

Rota stared for several long moments before she smiled, one of the few Bryn had seen. "Right answer. Ira's a good man and would never hurt a soul. I don't doubt he refused to come here and hurt us, so they hurt him and took his mother."

"We can't let his mother be harmed."

Rota snorted. "That woman is a battleax. Ira loves her and worries for her, but I've met the woman. She will badger and berate and belittle her captors until they are a mewling puddle of regret wishing for nothing more than to release her and never see her again. We worry about us...and Ira."

Bryn relaxed, sheathed her blade, and took a step back. She crossed her arms over her chest. "Time to explain what you meant by 'your life.' And why Mr. C wants it."

23

"Shit," Rota said.

She sagged into an armchair, plopped her feet on the ottoman, and heaved a sigh.

"Long day," Bryn said, taking a seat and propping up her feet, copying Rota, only realizing how tired she was when she sat down. It had been an exhausting, revelatory day. "Nice reinforcements you've created."

Rota closed her eyes and rested the back of her head on the chair. "You no doubt scoured the basement."

"Not every inch, but I saw the important bits." The glittering gold of the wings rose in her mind, the itch to put them on still strong. "You're certainly ready for a siege."

"I built it to hold against the horde, not humans."

Bryn sucked in a breath, all thoughts of snark gone. "You hate us that much?"

Rota opened her eyes but stared at the ceiling instead of looking at Bryn. "I don't hate the horde; I'd say it's the other way around. They failed Odin in the worst way; they shunned me when I refused to abandon my oath to him after he fell to Hades."

She finally lowered her head and pierced Bryn with a stare. "They will not take everything I've worked to build. They haven't the right."

Bryn gripped the arms of the chair, her heart sinking as her temper rose. "Even if it costs them their lives?"

Rota turned her gaze to the wall of windows, despite the view being blocked by metal. "They know what they must do to live; you know it too."

Bryn couldn't stop the impulse to touch the relic under her shirt.

"You've already begun, Bryn. I saw you when Rusty refused to fly for you. I saw you cry to Odin, ask for his forgiveness."

"Helena told me you saw me."

Rota smiled slightly. "That child sees far more than she should but understands less than half of it." She looked at Bryn again. "Turning to Odin is the only reason I let you stay; it's the only reason I allowed you to see what I have here. But don't mistake that for a softening of my stance on the horde. They made their bed, and they will die in it."

Temper coursed through Bryn, her face hot, sweat rolling down her back, but showing her anger wouldn't help the horde. There had to be a chink in Rota, a way to change her mind. For now, Bryn needed to cool off and keep Rota talking; blowing up wouldn't help, no matter how desperate she was growing.

"What's the story with Mr. C?"

Rota surged to her feet. "I need a beer. Want one?"

"Yeah, thanks."

Rota grabbed a couple bottles and handed one to Bryn before taking her seat again. "I've been fighting for him for years now. Working my way through the men, beating them, until now. These days it's getting harder to find a man willing to fight me. Mr. C has had to go far into the state to find fighters."

She took a deep drink. "A few months ago, he decided he wanted to take me deep underground for some seriously illegal fights. Lots of rich folks, lots of money."

"Aren't the fights he puts on now illegal?" Bryn asked, picking on a corner of the paper label on the bottle.

"Sure, but he's greased the right palms long enough to get away with it. What I'm talking about is as far underground as it gets. I'm talking about death matches."

Bryn slowly set her beer down then leaned forward in her chair. "He wants you to fight to the death for him?"

Rota nodded. "In the worst way."

"Is this why his sons broke into the Aries home?"

"I don't think so," Rota said softly, deep in thought as she also picked at her beer label, mimicking Bryn. "That's new. But I suspected Mr. C and his sons would get around to it eventually. Aries is very wealthy and very much *not* a fan of Mr. C."

"Mr. C knows you are friends with the family?"

"Oh, yes."

"Why did you get involved with the fighting at all?"

Rota drained her beer and set the empty bottle down. She linked her fingers. "Aries had given me a lot of money to build this place. I needed to pay him back and I wanted to do it fast."

"You're the family's protector; wasn't that enough to earn you the money?"

"They would have been fine with that; I'm the one who wouldn't take the money as a gift. I don't like owing anyone." Rota waved a hand. "Anyway, fighting allowed me to make pots of money. Unfortunately, I'm too good; Mr. C has gotten ambitious."

"Thus, the death matches. Seems like his ambition has gotten the best of him."

Rota drummed her fingers on the chair arm. "Seems someone triggered him."

Bryn watched her closely, saw the accusation. "Seems like you think it was me."

"Seems like you're going to help me fix this."

Bryn grinned, her adrenaline spiking.

"Can we go now?" she asked, jumping up.

"Can't leave the horses alone."

"Yes, you can," Ira said, leaning on the entrance to the great room. "I'll make sure they're not harmed."

Rota stood. "You can barely stand, my friend, much less fight."

He pushed off the wall and stood tall, unlike the hunched mess he was a short time ago. "They have my mom; you get her back and I'll make sure your horses aren't hurt."

Bryn waited for Rota to decide, eager to move, to go on the offensive instead of remaining defensive only. It didn't take as long as she thought it would considering the level of trust Rota would have to give the man.

"Okay, Ira." Rota walked up to him and touched one of his arms. "Come."

She led him, with Bryn following closely, to Rota's bedroom.

"Rota?" Bryn asked, surprised the woman would trust Ira with access to the basement.

But Rota didn't answer, nor did she lift the end of the bed. Instead, she opened her closet, walked to the armoire in the very back, and opened it, the weapons display impressive.

"You can handle guns? Rifles? Blades?" she asked Ira.

Ira ducked his head to enter the closet and joined Rota. He touched several of the pieces. "Yes."

Rota pulled out the drawers. "Ammunition is here."

Ira nodded.

"You know my number. Call me if there's any sign of trouble." Rota touched his arm again. "I'm counting on you."

He covered her hand entirely with his huge paw. "I'm counting on you."

Rota pulled away. "Let's go."

She left the bedroom.

Bryn turned to go with her, but Ira gently took her arm, stopping her. "Bryn?"

She let him pull her close.

He lifted her hands, one in each of his. "Please be careful. The Caldwell family needs to end you. They won't stop until you're dead."

"Is that the order you refused? To kill me?"

Ira stared into her eyes, his beautiful, hazel irises growing black as his pupils dilated. "I'm not a man to hurt people, though most think that because I'm so big, I'm inclined to do so. I would never kill unless it was a last resort. But you...I could never harm you."

He lifted her right hand and gently kissed her palm, then did the same with her left palm, his eyes never leaving hers.

Her mouth dropped open, too stunned to say anything. She trembled with a need she'd never felt before, the desire to fall into him nearly overwhelming.

"Bryn!" Rota said from deeper in the house.

Bryn pulled her hands free from Ira's then threw herself into his chest, wrapped her arms around his neck, which was no small feat, and gave him a quick kiss on the mouth before running after Rota.

She left the house, striding with a purpose now that she'd decided what had to be done. But instead of the coming mission, Bryn's mind lingered on the feel of Ira's mouth under hers, his huge, solid body, his words of reverence, foreign in her world, in her life.

The slam of the truck door and the start of the engine brought her back.

"We're not taking any weapons?" Bryn asked, climbing into the truck. "Seems foolish."

Rota drove away from her home, accelerating down the dark road. "We have a stop to make first."

They raced through the night until they reached the Aries home.

"What are we doing here?"

"Locking down the house when we leave so no one can get inside but me. It's a little extra security I set up with the family."

Rota parked and jumped out of the truck.

"Why wasn't the security in place before?"

"The boys and Helena and their nanny were staying here, and only Mr. Aries and I have the codes to lock down and stand down."

"That seems...excessive."

"After what you saw in the basement?" Rota asked, opening the front door and letting Bryn inside.

"Good point. Speaking of..."

"Come," Rota said, cutting her off.

She strode through the house to the kitchen.

Bryn had been in it before, but she'd been in too much of a hurry to take in the scale of the modern, gleaming space; it was a tribute to the excess only the wealthiest could afford. Like the rest of the house. Maybe she should approach Aries himself to help the horde. The family had the money to make them comfortable and maybe she could use his influence with Rota. Something to think about.

Rota entered a huge, U-shaped pantry. Two doors, the open space wrapped around a central, stationary set of shelves with drawers below. The other three walls were configured the same.

"Damn, these stores could feed the entire horde for a month," Bryn said, more than a little peeved.

Rota didn't respond. Instead, she reached behind a row of canned beans and pressed something, causing a deep *thunk*.

She pulled on the short side of the shelves until there was an opening wide enough for her to pass through. Then she disappeared.

"Another secret passage?" Bryn mumbled under her breath.

A light came on illuminating a set of narrow stairs going down.

"Does this go to the basement?" Bryn asked.

"Yes, but a separate room. You can't access the rest of the basement from here," Rota said before trotting down.

Bryn followed more slowly. Reaching the bottom of the stairs, she saw the open door; Rota had already entered.

Bryn slid inside and stopped cold. This day of surprises just wasn't going to stop. The Aries family had an armory. There was nothing else to call the cavernous space before her.

"What the hell does Aries need with all this?" Bryn asked, running her hands over an armored Humvee.

"He's an industrialist with his hands in a lot of pots, some a bit more questionable than others. He has a private security force—"

"And they are where instead of here protecting his family and home?" Bryn asked, interrupting her.

"They travel with him."

A sharp stab of anger stopped Bryn in her tracks. "What could possibly be more important than his family? His blood?"

Rota turned around, her jaw set, her full lips pressed hard into a thin line. "Getting home to them."

She pressed her thumb against a small pad. The light turned green, and she opened the door.

Bryn peered inside and gasped at the sheer number of weapons.

But Rota didn't pull down any gun. Instead, she pulled open a drawer and lifted out a dark gray catsuit. Long sleeves, legs that went to the ankle and a neckline that covered the entire neck to the jaw, the suit looked sheer; it certainly looked lightweight. She held up the suit and studied Bryn from head to toe.

"What's that for?" Bryn asked. "You have a tutu to go with it? We gonna scare them with our ninja ballerina moves?"

She snorted.

Rota tossed the catsuit to Bryn and took out another one. "Take off your clothes."

"What?"

Rota quickly stripped. "Put the suit on against your skin then get dressed again."

"Okaaay."

Bryn followed Rota's lead, surprised at the suit's close fit and comfort. Rota walked out of the room, holding the door for Bryn to follow her.

Bryn swept an arm around the room. "What are you doing? There are weapons here and you're taking nothing? We're facing Mr. C and his sons with nothing more than long johns? Long johns that don't even have a butt flap? What if I have to go to the bathroom?"

Rota walked away and disappeared up the stairs.

Bryn released the door and it shut behind her before she could change her mind and grab a weapon or five. "Damn it."

"Come on, Valkyrie!" Rota shouted.

Bryn jogged after the horsemaster. "Well, shit."

24

R
ota pulled into the far corner of the parking lot behind the warehouse and stopped her truck, studying the closed loading bays. "The back door has little security."

She lifted the center console, dug deep, and pulled out a slingshot and a leather bag.

Bryn had held her tongue while Rota had secured the Aries house—admittedly she was impressed by the growls and *clunks* that rang out in the night, the house vocalizing as it shut down as if it were a living thing. She'd remained silent while Rota had driven them to the fight club because Rota was sure Mr. C would be there, as would Ira's mother. She'd even kept her snark under wraps while Rota had explained that Mr. C wouldn't sully his own home with all this mess. But...

"A slingshot? Are you kidding me?"

Rota turned in her seat. "Do you ever shut up?"

"Do you ever answer questions?"

"I answered plenty earlier. As for this," she said, holding up the child's toy, "just watch."

She opened the leather bag and removed a good-sized, steel shot. She rolled down her window, put the bead in the slingshot, drew the band back, and aimed.

Rota released the band, and a light went out. One after another, she put out several lights, giving them a ring of darkness to shield the truck.

"Okay, that's nice," Bryn said.

"Just wait." Rota filled her pockets with the shot and left the truck. "Don't lock it."

Bryn nodded and followed Rota through the parking lot as she continued killing the lights.

Then Rota stopped at a sports car and squatted, giving her cover.

"What are we doing?" Bryn whispered.

"Going for the security cameras."

Rota rested her arm on the car, aimed, and fired. The camera on the right sagged. She took out the left camera and slipped the slingshot in her back pocket. She removed a lock pick set from her other back pocket.

"Going old school," Bryn said, whispering.

"All business in the front and almost no tech in the back," Rota said, concentrating on the lock until it clicked open.

"What's the plan?" Bryn asked, a little antsy that Rota hadn't said a word about breaking in.

She'd been ready to march in the front door, no pretense, no hiding.

"I'm going to make Mr. C understand he needs to stop."

Rota took off down a dark, narrow hall that ran the length of the back of the place. This part of the warehouse had been sectioned off from the main space and divided into multiple offices until it resembled a rabbit warren, all twisty and closed off.

"But, like, how?" Bryn asked, persisting.

Rota kept striding, ignoring the question, until they reached a cross hall.

"You know your way around here?" Bryn asked.

Rota held up a hand.

Bryn pressed her back against the wall, hugging the sliver of shadow.

Mr. C bulled his way down the hall, followed by his two sons, but no guards. The men passed the hall where Rota and Bryn hid, too deep in their conversation to notice.

"What do you mean you can't get inside the Aries house?" Mr. C bellowed.

"It's locked up tighter than ma's drawers," one of the sons said, Asshole or Idiot, Bryn couldn't tell.

But she could tell the sound of a hard slap when she heard it, and the grunt of pain.

"You can disrespect those girls you run with, but never your mama. Understand me, boy?"

Rota glanced at Bryn. Bryn widened her eyes, but said nothing. What could you say about such a fucked-up code?

The men walked on, heading in the direction of the grand office with the grandiose desk and "throne."

Rota blocked Bryn from coming around her and charging to the office. "Wait a second."

"What for?" Bryn asked in a whisper.

The sound of boots hitting the floor stopped Bryn. She pulled back and waited as two guards walked over to join Mr. C.

"Five to two. I like those odds," Bryn said.

"We're just here to talk. No fighting, no killing."

"Unless they start it."

Rota tilted her head. "If they do, we finish it right here. But there's something else I want that won't be accomplished by taking them out now. So, follow my lead." One of Rota's eyebrows rose. "Can you do that, or do I go in there alone?"

Bryn rolled her eyes for an answer.

"Let's go," Rota said.

She turned the corner and started down the hall.

"Oh," Bryn said under her breath, hustling to catch up.

Rota walked quickly to the closed double doors, pivoted, then side-kicked the right door open. The door slammed against the guard behind it, knocking him to the ground. The second guard turned to Rota and reached inside his suit coat.

She spun and slammed her heel into his jaw.

The man dropped.

"Just so," Bryn said under her breath.

"Get their weapons," Rota said.

Bryn took guns and knives off the two men then stowed the blades in her boots and disassembled the guns before tossing the parts down the hall. She closed the doors and stood in front of them, her arms crossed over her chest, flashing a smug smile at the remaining trio.

There's a new guard in town.

Mr. C sat back down and smiled, but his rage couldn't be hidden so easily; the red flush creeping out from under his starched collar spoke volumes. "Rota and Valkyrie. Just the pair I've been wanting to talk to."

With that, he did relax, his elbows on the arms of his chair, his fingers steepled. His two sons, however, quivered with the need to pull the triggers of the guns they pointed at the two women.

Mr. C slammed a hand down on his desk. "Put those guns away. I'll not have you bring more trouble down on us, especially killing. Even though it would be justified with the breaking and entering."

He focused on the two women to emphasize his point. His sons obeyed, but hatred shone through their compliance.

Rota waited a beat before speaking. "The answer is yes."

Bryn turned her attention to the horsemaster. "What?"

Rota ignored her. "But I have some demands."

Mr. C watched her, his eyes slowly narrowing as if trying to decide if she was serious. Finally, he waved her forward. "Take a seat."

Bryn leaned forward.

"What are you doing?" she said, her voice low, her question urgent.

Again, Rota ignored her. She sat in the chair and crossed her legs, her hands folded in her lap as if she hadn't a care in the world. Or a care for her life.

"You'll fight for me…in Denver," Mr. C said.

Bryn clenched her fists and fought the urge to hurl a knife into Mr. C's heart.

"Yes. In return, you will release Ira's mother to me tonight."

He studied her for a long time, his expression flat. "Done."

"And," Rota continued, "you will leave everything I consider mine untouched;

that includes the Aries family. No more threats, no more break-ins, no more target practice."

Mr. C smiled.

"One last thing. Ira and his mother are mine as well."

Mr. C stopped smiling. His lips thinned and turned white. "Fine, I agree. Here are my demands: You will fight and win for me. You will not go back to your ranch tonight or any other night until the first match is fought. I can't have my prize fighter bailing on me. Last, you'll drop the charges against my boys. Tomorrow. If you renege on any of this, I'll kill you myself and destroy everything you've built, starting with your horses and your ranch and ending with the entire Aries family. I will wipe all of you out of existence. Got that?"

Bryn trembled with frustration, the heat building so high she couldn't stop a hiss.

Rota threw up a hand to stay Bryn's temper, her outrage. "We have a deal."

25

Bryn's breath exploded out of her. "I need to talk to you, Rota. Now!"

"Seems your girl needs a moment," Mr. C said, his voice a satisfied croon. "You can go outside, but leave the doors open. No going out of my sight, or the deal's off and the war's on."

Rota slowly rose and walked out of the office, followed immediately by Bryn.

"I thought the plan was to make them stop, not have you go in the ring and fight to the death. What are you doing?" Bryn asked, shoving Rota against the wall.

Rota's face remained expressionless. "I'm protecting my family."

Bryn backed off and shook her head. "So, you *are* familiar with the concept of family. You *are* willing to do what it takes to protect them." She curled her lip. "You *are* just like me."

"Your family has made a choice that's now leading to their destruction; mine has not. Your family could easily stop the loss, the pain; mine cannot. Your family is willing to hand off responsibility for their lives to someone else…you; I am not."

Bryn slashed the edge of her open hand through the air. "You would rather fight and kill for that monster than stand up to him for the good of your family? You think they want your life as a killer or your death on their conscience?"

"Perhaps not," Rota said, her nostrils flaring. "But I do what I must."

Bryn grabbed the front of Rota's shirt and jerked her close.

"If you kill, Odin will turn his back on you just like he did the horde," she said, her voice low. "You'll doom the Valkyrie to extinction. The horses will never fly again."

Rota cocked her head. "Why do you continue to lay their survival at my feet? *They* are responsible for themselves; not me, not you. Until you get that through your thick, stubborn head, you will be doomed to disappointment."

Bryn shoved her back with both hands. "Damn you then."

Mr. C snapped his fingers. "Get Ira's mother and show them out. Rota, here."

"Damn it, Rota, no!"

Rota turned her back on Bryn and walked over to Mr. C. She turned and only then looked at Bryn again, her expression passive.

Asshole and Idiot shoved Bryn down the hall.

"We could take them now, Rota! End this!"

Rota said nothing, did nothing.

Idiot shoved her again.

Bryn whipped around and shoved him back. "Touch me again and I will take you apart."

His eyes widened and he backed up a step.

"Bryn!" Rota said, her voice low but booming.

Bryn snarled at the two men before turning her attention to the woman.

"Leave here, now," Rota said, her order not to be challenged.

Bryn hesitated, the desire to fight nearly outweighing the need to listen to Rota despite disagreeing with her. Rota must have a plan. The question was: Did she trust that Rota knew what she was doing?

Finally, Bryn grunted and snapped her fingers under the men's noses, the insult intended.

The men led her to another room, locked from the outside. They opened the door and Bryn got to witness an impressive display of feral woman.

The old lady lunged up; the chair she'd been seated in still attached to her by duct tape. She charged the closest man, and the pair went down in a tangle of legs and gnashing teeth—her teeth and his legs. She bit them over and over, mangling every fleshy bit she could reach.

The man screamed and slapped at the woman, but she was relentless.

"I like her," Bryn said.

"Oh, just shut up and help me get them apart before I have to shoot her," Idiot said.

Bryn stepped up to the woman, grabbed her by the half-undone bun and pulled her head back. "Stop, now, or I'll rip out your hair."

The woman snapped her teeth, but she couldn't reach Bryn.

Bryn released her hair then gripped the woman's surprisingly muscular arms. She grunted as she pulled the woman back into a sitting position and, pulling a dagger from her boot, cut the duct tape, freeing her.

"We're getting out of here," Bryn told her.

"Where's Ira? Where's my son?"

"Safe. I'll take you to him."

Bryn slipped the dagger back in her boot, shoved Mr. C's sons to the side, and waved for Ira's mother to follow her. "I know my way out."

The men followed the two women through the warehouse and out the front door, where they left them alone and retreated inside, locking the door.

Ira's mother rubbed her bruised wrists and rolled her head. "Those boys are idiots."

Bryn started walking. "No argument here. What's your name?"

"Mary Lynne. You?"

"Bryn." She picked up the pace until they reached Rota's truck. "Get in."

She lowered the driver's visor and the keys fell into her lap.

Mary Lynne climbed in. "You serious about Ira? He's okay?"

Bryn started the engine then drove out of the parking lot and away from the fight club. "They beat the hell out of him, but he's healing up fine, and fast too. I'm taking you to him now."

"Those no-good bastards. They've gone too far this time."

Bryn studied the woman's profile, her smooth skin, the cool set to her eyes.

This wasn't just some badger mom worried about her child. Something else was going on here, but Bryn couldn't see it. Not yet.

A tingle of concern worked its way down her spine. Whom to trust? She only knew Rota and Helena. Ira was no threat; she felt that to her marrow. But this woman warranted watching.

The pair fell silent. When they reached the ranch, Mary Lynne jumped out of the truck and trotted to the front door, waiting for Bryn to open it.

As soon as she did, Mary Lynne stepped inside.

"Ira? Boy? Where are you?"

"Mother!"

Ira race-walked to her, and she hugged him gently.

Pulling back, she looked him over. "By damn, they did give you a walloping. You gonna be okay?"

Ira gave her a lopsided grin and looked over her shoulder at Bryn. "Bryn patched me up good. I already feel much better. You okay? They didn't hurt you, did they?"

"Nah, you know I can take care of myself." Mary Lynne gently patted his unbruised cheek. "Speaking of which, can a woman get a shower around here? I need to get the stink of that place off me. And clean clothes."

Bryn fought not to laugh at the bossy woman. "There's a guest bath down the left hall. I'll bring you some clothes."

"I get done, I'll cook us up a hearty meal. Best thing for healing, next to a good night's sleep."

She marched down the hall and disappeared inside the bathroom.

"I know warriors who aren't as tough as her," Bryn said.

Ira grinned, but the usual soft expression in his eyes was gone, replaced by an awareness Bryn hadn't associated with him. "That she is." Then his focus softened, and he hunched a little, as if falling back into a role. He glanced at Bryn. "So, what do we have in the way of food?"

Curious.

He walked to the kitchen. "And where's Rota?"

26

"Rota gave herself to Mr. C to free me?" Mary Lynne asked, sitting back from the table.

Bryn sipped the beer Ira had found. "I don't know how much Rota wants known, but we're past the need for secrecy here. Besides, Ira probably knows far more about Mr. C and his business than Rota does. Mr. C wants Rota to fight in underground clubs…to the death."

"Rota always says no," Ira said.

"Until tonight," Bryn said. "In exchange for fighting, you were released, and this ranch, the Aries family, and you and your mother are protected."

Mary Lynne threw her napkin onto the table. "That's just stupid. He's just one man with two no-good sons."

"And plenty of money and influence. His sons already injured four of Rota's horses and they threatened to kill the rest. Not to mention burn down everything Rota's worked for. I'm furious with her, but I understand why she did it."

"This wouldn't have happened if you hadn't shown up, causing trouble," Mary Lynne said.

Ira shook his head hard. "No, this would have happened anyway. Bryn may have gotten Mr. C riled up, but it's not her fault. He's been wanting Rota to fight for the big money for a long time."

Mary Lynne patted his forearm. "Always seeing the good, aren't you?"

He smiled softly and ducked his head.

Bryn pushed back from the table. "I've got horses to feed."

Mary Lynne stood, followed quickly by Ira, though he leaned a little to one side favoring his bruised ribs. "My boy needs to rest. Got beds for us?"

Bryn thought about putting Mary Lynne in Rota's room but decided against it. The access to the basement compound needed to be guarded by her.

"There are two king beds in one guest room or one of you can sleep in Ashton's room. He's probably staying in the barn tonight, given all the excitement."

"Who's Ashton?" Mary Lynne asked.

"The head horse around here."

"And he has a bedroom?" Ira's mama asked, her incredulity pitching her voice high.

Bryn laughed. "Something, isn't it? I'll show you the rooms and you can decide."

"Oh, no deciding needed," the woman said, laughing. "Ira snores like a freight train; I'll take the room farthest away from him."

"That'll be Ashton's room."

Bryn gave them the tour and Mary Lynne agreed Ashton's room was the right choice, though she did grumble that Rota was batshit crazy for having a horse living in her house.

"I'll stay in the room with the two beds," Ira said. "Can I come with you to feed the horses?"

"You sure you don't need to lie down? You've had a helluva day."

"I'll sleep better if I know the lay of the place."

Bryn inclined her head then headed down the passageway to the barn.

"Where are Helena and her brothers?" Ira asked. "I thought they'd be here."

"Rota has them stashed somewhere safe."

"Where?" he insisted.

Bryn stopped and turned on him. "Why do you want to know?"

Ira shrugged one shoulder. "I like Helena."

Bryn snorted. "She's too young for you, pal."

Even in the lower light, Bryn saw him blush.

"Not like that," he said. "She's always been kind to me. Like a little sister."

"I said they're safe. Leave it at that. If you want to help, find out everything you can about these death matches. Where are they? When? The more we can find out and fast, the better chance we have to help Rota."

"Sounds like she made up her mind. You sure she wants help?"

"There's more at stake than just this place and her friends if she kills in the death matches. She may not want help, but she's going to get it. Question is: Are you going to help me?"

They walked a few feet in silence before Ira spoke. "I don't like going against Rota's wishes, and I don't know about these other stakes, but I don't want to see her risk her life. If you have a computer, I know Mr. C's passwords. I can find out which fight he's signed her up for."

Bryn opened the door to the food room of the first stall and started portioning out the mare's grain. "All of the passwords?"

"I have them memorized."

"Cell phone too?"

Ira gave her a big grin.

"Damn, man. Let's finish this and get to snooping."

* * *

"Ira, you've got some unplumbed depths," Bryn said hours later.

"Mr. C isn't as careful as he should be," Ira said, rubbing his eyes like a five-year-old.

"And that only helps us." She stood and gently squeezed his shoulder. "Rota has bought us a reprieve from attack, and you've given us a head start on the fight. Let's get some sleep. We have a lot of planning to do tomorrow."

Ira closed Rota's laptop. "Do you think we should let Mr. Aries know what's happening?"

"He's not here; what can he do? He's flying home in a couple days anyway."

Ira limped down the hall to his bedroom. He stopped, a hand on the doorknob. "If it were my family, I would want to know."

He walked inside and closed the door.

Bryn ran her hands through her hair and sagged from fatigue. "Well, hell."

He's right; Aries needs to know the shitstorm he's flying into.

She sat at Rota's computer and searched the contacts list, expecting to email the man, but when she clicked on his name, Facetime opened.

Bryn blinked. She'd never used the program, but before she could close it, a man appeared.

"Rota," he said, before frowning. "Who the fuck are you?"

Handsome wasn't a strong enough descriptor for Aries. Short, blond hair with a few grays at the temple, a sculpted face the gods would be happy to claim, and clear, light blue eyes like a high-altitude, glacier-fed lake—the man was stunning. And pissed.

"I'm Bryn. I'm a Valkyrie."

His thick eyebrows rose high. "And Rota let you live?"

Bryn couldn't stop her grin. "I've grown on her."

"So, Valkyrie Bryn, why are you calling me instead of Rota?"

Bryn quickly ran through what had happened that day and what Rota had done to secure everyone's safety. With each moment, Aries's face grew darker.

"That sonofabitch," he said when Bryn finished. "Are you sure my children are safe?"

"Rota is sure and she's the only one who knows where they are. She didn't even tell me. Rota also secured your home so Mr. C can't get inside in case he ignores his agreement with her. We know there's something he's after; Odin knows there's plenty for him to plunder."

Aries stared through her for a second, fully understanding what she was saying. "Got an eyeful, did you?"

"I saw enough to know there's much at stake. Far more than someone like Mr. C could possibly imagine. Something very dark and dangerous that can't be allowed loose in the world," she said carefully.

"I see," he said just as carefully, acknowledging her words without shedding any light. "I'll be calling for my jet as soon as we're done here. In the meantime, are you alone at the ranch?"

"I have Ira and his mother here. Their safety was also part of the bargain Rota made. We're secure here."

He cocked his head. "But that's not your plan, is it? To stay behind her fortifications or trust Mr. C's word."

"No, it's not."

His jaw muscles clenched. He nodded. "Good. I have resources of my own. I'm going to send them to you tonight. The code word is 'The Furious.'"

Bryn couldn't stop her involuntary jerk of recognition. "Odin."

"Who else? Expect them within a couple hours."

"I don't have the room to house a bunch of people, and I won't allow them access to the horses."

He smiled, the lopsided grin devastating. "They know better than to ask." He looked past the screen and nodded at someone. "I have to go. I look forward to meeting you, Valkyrie. Stand true." He raised a fist. "To the Allfather."

The call ended before Bryn could respond. She sat back in the chair and pressed her right fist over her heart. "To Odin."

Well, hell. She could like this Aries guy, even if she did have a butt load of questions and planned on giving him a slap down for keeping a Black Zodiac on ice.

A soft knock on the door brought her out of her thoughts.

"Bryn?"

"Yeah, Ira, come in."

He cracked the door open, his eyes closed.

"I'm dressed, Ira. You can open your eyes."

He entered the bedroom, his face red again.

The man seriously couldn't help himself. *Adorable.*

"I talked with a friend I can trust." He handed her a piece of paper. "Mr. C already has a fight set up for tomorrow night. In Denver."

"So soon?" She took the paper from him. "I spoke with Aries."

Ira's impressive eyebrows rose so high they disappeared under his hair. "And?"

"One, he's getting on his jet now. Two, he's sending security here to help us. They should be here in a couple hours."

"That's good." He looked away for a moment. "What are we going to do about Rota?"

She rose from the chair, took Ira by the arm, and walked him to the door. "We're going to get some sleep then plan what to do tomorrow."

He nodded then left for his room.

Bryn shut the door and stared at the address he'd given her for a long time.

27

The night passed too quickly, Bryn's few hours of sleep too restless to give her much relief from her fatigue. Despite that, she had a plan. Or maybe she'd been restless because of her plan. Not a good one, but one that would ensure Rota's survival.

The security force that Aries had sent was no joke. They were big and armed and many in number, warriors all. Their leader had barely said anything after asking for the password; his team had formed a perimeter around the compound and disappeared into the darkness. Bryn would never have guessed they were there had she not known it.

Mary Lynne was already awake and busy cooking breakfast when Bryn dragged herself to the coffee pot for some much-needed go-go juice.

"Girl, your bags have bags," the older woman said, sliding bacon and eggs and hash browns onto a plate that she laid on the table. She pointed to it. "Sit. Eat."

Bryn sipped her coffee and sighed, hoping the caffeine would kick in quickly. "I need to feed the horses."

"Ira's already on it."

"But—"

"My boy is a quick study. He saw you feed last night. He didn't forget."

"He's a man of hidden depths, isn't he?" Bryn asked, sliding into a chair and pulling the laden plate closer.

Mary Lynne snorted and took a seat across from Bryn, digging into her food. "You have no idea."

Bryn set down her mug and ate, the rich, heavy meal just what she needed to fuel herself.

"What's the plan for Rota?" Mary Lynne asked.

The woman wasn't one to mince words.

Bryn hesitated. How much to say? What did she really know of these people? Rota knew them, trusted them enough to allow them to stay here, but Bryn didn't.

She settled for the simplest truth. "I have to get inside the fight club tonight. It's the only way I can be there in case she needs me."

Mary Lynne put down her fork, wiped her mouth with her napkin, then sat back. "You think Mr. C's people will allow you to interfere?"

"I'll not leave her alone."

The woman picked up the empty plates and took them to the sink. She turned around and leaned against the counter. "Ira will go with you."

Bryn shook her head. "He's not healed yet; he's of no use to me if he can't fight."

Mary Lynne poured herself a cup of coffee, drowned it with sugar, then joined Bryn at the table again. "You ever heard of Solomon?"

Bryn snorted. "Tear a baby in half Solomon?"

"Yes, that one."

"I've heard of him, but what's he got to do with Ira?"

Mary Lynne took a long sip and a longer stare at Bryn, as if trying to decide how much she would say. Seemed Bryn wasn't the only one having those internal discussions.

"If you haven't figured it out by now, Ira is special."

Every mother would say the same about their child.

"I heard that," Mary Lynne said.

Bryn stiffened. "What?"

Mary Lynne pointed a finger at Bryn's face and twirled it in a circle. "It's all over your face. You think I'm being a mother."

Bryn burst out laughing. "You got me there."

Mary Lynne chuckled. "I'm that kind of mother, but I'm also right. Ira is descended from one of King David's priests. For centuries, the name Ira has been given to the men in his family. Starting from the reign of King David to King Solomon and on and on until my Ira."

Bryn's humor vanished.

"Is he a paranorm?" she asked, interested to see if the woman understood the word.

Ira's mother shook her finger. "You think to trip me up, but I know exactly what paranorm means, and that they have emerged from the InBetween only recently."

She dropped her hand and looked past Bryn, her eyes glazing over as if seeing something other than the interior of Rota's home.

"I've kept Ira away from the InBetween but close to the Aries family because it was safer for him. Aries is strong, wealthy; he can afford to give Ira the help he'll need. At least that's what I thought," she said, her voice softening, "until I met you."

Bryn recoiled. "What the hell do you mean by that?"

"That's enough," Ira said from across the room. He joined them at the table and took a seat. "Don't scare the poor woman."

Bryn did a doubletake. "Ira?"

Every bruise was gone. She could see from the tight tee shirt that he'd removed the bandage around his ribs.

"I heal fast," he said simply.

"I heal fast and I'm a Valkyrie," she said, "but even our kind doesn't heal that fast."

"I told you he was special."

"I'm starting to get that," Bryn said, studying the man.

"To change the subject," Ira said, his handsome face red again. "What's the plan?"

Bryn leaned forward, her elbows on the table. "I'm going to crash the event. If I'm there, I can help Rota if she needs it."

Ira flattened his hands on the table. "If you're going to be there, so am I."

"I need you to take care of the horses."

He shook his head, his adorable, wavy hair falling into his eyes. He pushed it back. "Mother can take care of them; we'll write out the instructions."

"I don't need your help, Ira. Stay here."

He watched her, his jaw set until even Mary Lynne started to twitch. "You may be used to fighting your own battles, Bryn, but you're not going in that place without me."

"And if I leave you behind?"

He grinned for the first time. "I'll follow you."

"Mary Lynne?" Bryn asked, sure the woman would want her son to remain safe.

The woman shook her head. "Ira is a protector, just like you. He goes with you."

"Aw, hell." Bryn pushed away from the table and rose. "Then we need to get ready and tell the security team we're leaving."

* * *

The head of the security team wasn't happy, but there was nothing he could do to stop them.

Bryn started for Rota's truck, but Ira put a hand on her shoulder.

"I'll drive."

"Because you're the man?" she asked, her hackles up.

He smiled softly, his patience seemingly knowing no bounds. "Because I know the way."

She reluctantly handed the keys to him and climbed in the passenger seat. "You better be glad you're cute. Otherwise, I'd have to take you down."

Ira burst out laughing.

"You'd be the first woman to accomplish that," he said, pulling away from the compound.

Bryn grinned and turned her upper body to look at him. "Oh? And how many have tried?"

Just as she expected, his face flushed bright red. The man would combust one of these days. Until he did, she'd have some fun.

Ira kept his eyes on the road. "Enough."

"Do we need to go over the plan again?" she asked, changing the subject.

"Get inside. Wait for Rota's fight. Help her."

"It's a long drive, big guy. Maybe expound a bit."

"I'm not a big talker."

"I got that."

"We have a way in," he continued. "The rest requires winging it."

Bryn's shoulders twitched. She rolled them and sat back, facing forward again. "How exactly did you heal so quickly?"

He remained silent for so long Bryn thought he was refusing to answer the question.

Finally, he cleared his throat. "I was given a gift, one passed down to every Ira."

"And you'll have this gift…"

"Until my death, at which time it'll be passed to my son, Ira."

She snorted. "Sounds like you need to get busy making babies."

He turned his head and stared at her. "Yes, I do."

She returned his stare for a beat.

"Stow that thinking and pay attention to the road," she finally said, pointing to the windshield, desperate to get out of the suggestive stare she'd fallen into.

He flashed her a grin again, as if knowing she'd understood his implication and had been discomfited by it.

"Cheeky bastard," she muttered, sinking into her seat.

Ira chuckled.

Bryn crossed her arms and brooded. Nothing and no one were as they seemed, and she was no closer to helping the horde. That would change as soon as they rescued Rota and dealt with Mr. C and his sons. Even if she had to use her last resort and steal one or more of Rota's flying horses to do it.

28

The parking lot around the abandoned mall was packed with expensive cars and SUVs, yet there was no sign announcing an event. Ira drove around the perimeter of the place, the collection of buildings built in a rectangle with a glass dome in the center.

"Did your friend tell you which door to use?" Bryn asked, craning her neck to look for security.

"Cheaper By The Dozen." He stared at each door as he slowly drove past them. "There should be a sign."

They drove around back and found a few cars parked there, all of them older and far cheaper than the group on the other side of the mall.

"There," Bryn said, pointing to a door.

Ira parked close. They trotted across the road and stood on either side of the entrance. Ira knocked softly.

The door opened and a red-haired man in a security guard uniform glanced at the two of them. "Hurry. The first fights have started."

"Not Rota," Bryn said, slipping past the man.

"No, she's not until later. You have time." He shut the door. "My debt to you is paid, Ira."

Ira offered his hand, and the two men shook. "In full, my friend."

The threesome started down the back hall.

"Tell us about the fighting cage," Bryn said. "Where it's located, how to get in."

"It's under the glass dome. The only way to get inside is the gate. Or the open top," the man said. "But you'd have to climb into the roof rafters and drop in."

"How far is the drop?" she asked.

"This is a three-story mall, and the dome goes even higher. That's shatter-both-legs-or-worse kind of far. I wouldn't recommend it."

Bryn nudged Ira with an elbow.

"Show us," Ira said quietly.

The man shrugged. "Your funeral."

He led them through a maze of back halls until he came to a door just outside the old security office. "It's locked."

Ira gripped the doorknob and yanked. The metal sheared, and the knobs fell to the floor. The door creaked open.

Bryn's jaw dropped at the show of strength. *Damn.*

Ira stepped inside. "It's dark."

The security guard raised his phone, the flashlight feature illuminating the hall. They walked a short distance, until the hall stopped at the base of narrow, metal stairs.

Ira's friend shone the light up. "Follow the stairs. They lead across the mall's ceiling to the edge of the dome and around it. You sure this is the way you want to go?"

Ira rested a hand on the man's shoulder. "Thanks for the help. We got it from here."

The man left them.

"After you," Ira said, gesturing to the stairs.

They climbed then eased their way across the narrow bridge that spanned the mall. By the time they reached the dome, they were at least forty-five feet, maybe more, above the first floor and the fenced fight cage.

Bryn sat and peered down at the combatants, the smell of blood and sweat already rank, the bellows of the crowd slamming into her.

"Blood lust has been a part of humanity since the beginning," Ira whispered in her ear. "We may seem more civilized these days, but it's just a façade."

"A façade that's absent here."

The smaller combatant jumped on the larger man's back, wrapped his arms around the man's head, and twisted hard. Bryn didn't have to hear the snap to see the impact of the broken neck. The beefy fighter dropped where he stood.

The crowd roared.

"Not bloody, but definitive," Bryn said.

"Doesn't this bother you?"

"The Valkyrie fight a lot; it's part of their training."

"To the death?"

"Never, especially not now."

"Why?"

She hesitated to go into it with him, but his gentle expression encouraged her to talk. "They're dying out. My people."

She watched the clean-up crew drag the dead man out while the man left standing strutted around the ring, celebrating his win.

"Why are they dying?"

"Rota says it's because the Valkyrie broke their oath to Odin. As a result the horses have stopped flying."

"Flying horses?"

She glanced at him. "So, you don't know everything."

"Not even close. I know the Valkyrie rode horses, and mythology says the horses flew, but it's real?"

"Oh, yes, but our horses have lost the ability to fly. Our lives are tied to our horses; what befalls them damns us. Rota's horses can fly."

"You came to get her help."

"And her horses. I came to save my people."

He rested his chin on the metal railing. "Seems your people should rededicate themselves to Odin."

"That's what Rota says. It's not that easy."

The crowd roared again. Another pair of combatants entered the ring; the gate shut behind them.

Bryn settled in, watching as pair after pair fought to the death, the crowd growing, in size and enthusiasm. Occasionally, a fight would break out among the spectators, but the burly security guards quickly broke them up. It wouldn't do to have the wealthy patrons bloodied; might close their fat purses.

The sun set. The fights grew more violent until the ring was a bloody mess, slippery in some spots, sticky in others, an additional handicap for the fighters.

Finally, the latest fight ended, the ring was cleared, and the lights dimmed.

"Ladies and gentlemen. We have reached the final match of the night. A special bout with a fighter new to us, but renowned in Aspen. I give you…Rota!"

Rota entered the ring, and the crowd screamed their approval.

"They really want to see a woman get killed, don't they?" Bryn asked.

Ira didn't speak, but she saw his hands tighten on the rail, his knuckles turning white. Bryn covered his closest hand with one of hers, offering comfort.

"Rota will not die," he said.

"I don't believe she'll lose, but killing will hurt her. It could even threaten the horses' ability to fly," she said, her voice dropping off, horrified at the thought. Her hand tightened on Ira's. "I can't let her kill her opponent. I can't take the chance."

Ira turned his head and stared at her. "You mean 'we' don't you?"

The gate opened again, silencing her.

"A special request has been made and granted!" the announcer said. "Make your bets, ladies and gentlemen! Now!"

A line of movement snaked through the crowd. A man entered the ring, then another, and another, on and on until seven men stood opposite Rota, their hands clenched, their knees slightly bent.

Bryn rose and leaned over the railing. "They can't do that."

Ira climbed to his feet. "They can here. No rules, remember?"

Rota stood in the ring, her body relaxed, studying the men.

"I have to get down there," Bryn said.

Ira put one of his huge hands on her arm and gripped it firmly. "Not yet. We go down there now, the fight could be forfeited. She has to fight alone, for as long as she can."

But if she kills...

"If she can't defeat them?"

"Then we help her. Rest assured, I'll not see her die."

Bryn nodded, her heart screaming to jump, but her head accepting he was right. She sat down and resigned herself to waiting.

Ira sat so close they were hip to hip; he wrapped an arm around her.

Bryn leaned into him, half of her focus on the ring, the other half, the woman half, soaking up his heat, relishing the scent she associated with him alone as the need to sink into him washed over her...

She sat up with a jerk. *No, no, no. Not happening.*

Ira dropped his arm. Bryn swore she heard him chuckle. Before she could fuss at him, the gate closed; the crowd surged closer to the chain-link. Some even slipped their fingers through the fencing and clung to it. A bell rang.

The men spread apart.

The crowd quieted, waiting for the first attack.

Bryn took a breath and held it.

29

Rota took a step forward and waited.

"That's a good tactic," Bryn said.

"Let your opponents come to you, watch them for weaknesses," Ira said.

"Exactly. Have you fought?"

"I avoid fighting at all costs."

Bryn stared at him. "Why are you here if you're not going to fight?"

The crowd yelled before Ira could answer. Bryn turned her attention back to the ring in time to see one of the men charge Rota. The woman stood still, but Bryn could see the tensing of her muscles, her arms slightly out from her body.

Rota waited until the man was almost on top of her before she stepped to the side and kicked his feet out from under him. He hit the floor and slid, hitting the cage wire hard. He crumpled into a ball and didn't move. Before Rota could reset, another man charged forward, but this one watched her closely.

Rota danced to the side again, but the man slowed his run and moved with her.

He swung a hard right hook. Rota leaned back to avoid the punch then sprung forward and drove into his chest, pushing him. He pummeled her back. She lifted him and slammed him down on the floor.

He scissored his legs and trapped her waist between them then started punching her face and chest. She grabbed his wrists and held them, their muscles straining, their faces red and sweaty. She roared and shoved, her strength and fury overpowering him.

Before she could subdue him, another man ran up and kicked her in the head, sending her off the man on the ground and into a heap.

"Damn it," Bryn yelled, her voice drowned out by the spectators.

She jumped to her feet again, ready to drop into the cage and stomp the men into the ground.

Ira reached out a hand and gripped her arm again. "Not yet."

Bryn struggled to free herself, but he was too strong. "Release me."

"Not until you settle. Give her a chance." He pointed to the men. "Look, they're waiting to see if Rota gets up."

"That's the least amount of decency they can offer."

"Bryn," Ira said.

She pursed her lips but sat again.

Rota's head rose off the floor. She shook it hard and climbed to her feet. Wiping her mouth with the back of her hand, she nodded to the men. One man stepped forward, his fists up.

Rota mirrored his stance.

"Now it's getting started," Ira said. "I've seen her fight dozens of times. It's like she has to go down once to warm up, then she's in it. I've never seen anyone fight like her."

"You've never seen the Valkyrie."

Rota and the man met in the middle and the blows started. Punch after punch, blood and sweat rolled down their faces and painted their skin. No matter how hard the man hit, Rota stood her ground until finally the man backed away, too exhausted to continue.

Another man stepped forward, his hands lower, his feet bare. He bounced from foot to foot, kicking and punching, Rota blocking and resting until the man made the mistake of getting too close. She threw an uppercut that sent him flying back. He hit the floor and stayed there.

"Six to go," Bryn said.

"She didn't kill the man. Still seven to go."

Bryn's stomach lurched. "Have you ever seen her kill an opponent?"

"Never."

Unease tickled the back of her neck, the growing surety that Mr. C had put multiple opponents in the ring with Rota to force her to kill to survive driving her to distraction. The man knew more than he should.

"This is wrong."

"Killing? Yeah, it is," Ira said.

Rota took down a second man, but he still lived. She staggered back a couple steps; the relentless punishment she was taking to avoid killing was wearing on her.

"No, I don't just mean one person killing another is wrong."

Ira shifted to face her. "You said the Valkyrie's existence is at risk if Rota kills. Care to explain?"

"Mythology says we chose warriors who were felled on the battlefield and took them to Valhalla to wait for Ragnarök, but that's not the whole story. We also took certain warriors that Odin picked, killing them so they could end up with the Allfather."

"I think I read that somewhere."

"But it's never been confirmed. I'm doing that now so you understand that for a Valkyrie to kill on her own is against Odin's express command. We can kill to save our own lives or each other, to save our horses, to save the innocent, but that's all."

Ira pointed to the fight below. "Seems she's fighting for her life."

"She chose to fight to the death."

"That's a pretty small distinction."

"No matter how small the difference, she's risking everything she's built."

"And risking the one chance the horde has to survive," Ira said.

"That too."

"You know this for sure?"

She shook her head. "No, not for sure. It's a gut feeling that I can't shake."

"Like Odin is talking to you?"

Bryn stared down at Rota fighting the men, his words ringing true. Maybe that's exactly what it was: Odin speaking to her, warning her. Rota couldn't be allowed to kill the men in the cage.

But I can. I can keep Rota from suffering Odin's wrath. I can save her, the horses, and the horde.

The crowd gasped, the change in their tone grabbing Bryn's attention. The door had opened. Two men stood blocking the exit: Mr. C's sons. They dropped knives of various sizes on the ground and quickly backed away, closing the gate, their grins evil.

Ira stood.

The seven men rushed to the weapons, each one getting a blade to wield, leaving Rota with nothing.

Bryn rose and gripped the railing until her knuckles blanched. "This is bad."

The armed men circled Rota. She looked around, crouched, and waited; there was nothing else for her to do.

"Rota killing them would be bad; Rota dying would be worse," Bryn whispered.

"It's time," Ira said, quietly.

The seven men slowly advanced, their blades ready. Bryn didn't say a word. She climbed onto the railing and watched as the men closed in on Rota. Ira stepped over the rail, only his heels on the edge of the platform.

"Time," Bryn finally said, releasing the railing, letting gravity do the work.

She dropped through the hole in the cage roof and landed hard on one knee, head bowed, right next to Rota.

The crowd's cheering sputtered to a stop. Silence reigned.

No more than a second later, the floor vibrated as Ira's massive body landed. Bryn and Ira rose as one then turned so their backs were to Rota.

The silence shattered. The crowd screamed. Those closest to the cage grabbed the chain-link and shook it.

Bryn hated every pampered, vicious wretch that found a thrill in blood sport. They had no idea the pain their pleasure wrought, or they didn't care. Either way, Bryn wished she could bloody every one of them.

"What the hell are you doing here?" Rota asked.

"We're here to keep you from losing your life, and Odin's favor."

Once over their surprise, the men advanced again.

"This isn't the agreement I made with Mr. C."

"You didn't agree to seven against one, did you?" Bryn asked.

"No."

"And you can't kill even one of these men." Bryn glanced over her shoulder. "Leave that to me."

"You'll never become a horsemaster if you do," Rota yelled at her.

"Shut up and fight. Leave the killing to me."

30

The first man to break charged at Bryn, knife poised to stab her in the heart. She readied herself, her focus on the tip and the hand holding it.

He didn't stop, didn't slow; he rushed forward without a plan, making it easy for Bryn to step to the side and grab his wrist with her left hand. She slammed the flat of her hand into his elbow, forcing it to bend. The point of his blade turned away from her and toward him.

His forward momentum caused him to impale his own chest with the knife, all the way to the hilt.

Bryn pulled the blade from his chest and kicked him in the abdomen, sending him to the edge of the ring to die.

The crowd yelled their approval.

"Ira, Rota, send them to me. I'll take them out," she ordered, her gut twisting at the sacrifice she had decided to make, and how easy it was to make it.

Two more men rushed them.

Rota and Ira intercepted them.

They fought with the men then put them down on the ground. Bryn dropped to her knees, wrestled one of the men's blades from his hand then stabbed both men in the heart simultaneously.

A groan started in the crowd as they realized their bets could be lost.

"Give me a blade!" Rota yelled.

Bryn handed the spare blade to Ira.

"Damn it!" Rota bellowed.

"No killing for you!" Bryn answered, readying for the next round.

The last four men moved in as one.

Ira and Bryn stood with Rota between them.

These last men proved not only that they had a brain, but that they'd watched the fight carefully, seeing Bryn's moves and that she was protecting Rota. They closed in but stayed out of range, circling, waiting, patient, unlike the other three fighters.

One lunged at Ira and swept his blade. Ira leaned back but didn't engage.

Bryn saw the four men glance at one another; they now understood that she should be their focus. *Just what I want.*

As if planned, the four men moved in on Bryn. One man pushed Rota back with the threat of his knife. A second feigned an attack, forcing Ira to focus on him, separating him from Bryn until she stood alone, surrounded.

Bryn braced herself, breathing deep to steady her mind, engaging her senses to help her feel the direction of the attacks as they came.

The man on her right took a step and slashed at her arm.

She leaned back and the man behind her cut her back. She flinched at the sharp, hot pain. It wasn't deep, not yet. They were like a wolf pack that would nip and claw from every direction, weakening their prey from a thousand bloody cuts until she staggered and fell and died.

Blood ran down her back. Bryn rolled her shoulders.

She heard a grunt behind her.

Rota had jumped on the man who'd cut Bryn, her legs wrapped around his waist, one of her arms around his neck, the other hand fighting to take the knife from him.

"Do not kill him," Bryn ordered.

Rota scowled, wrenched the knife out of the man's hand, then dropped from his back. She hit the ground and slashed at the back of one knee then the other, cutting his tendons.

He howled in pain and dropped to the floor, his blood flowing.

Down, but not dead.

Ira stepped up and backhanded one of the men away from Bryn.

The man slid several feet. Ira followed and fell on the man. One knee planted in the man's chest, he dropped the knife and broke the man's right forearm over his thigh like a piece of dried wood.

The crowd catcalled as the man screamed.

Ira stood, his feet on either side of the man's torso. "You done? Or do I have to break the other arm?"

The man held up his left hand and shook his head before tucking his broken arm into his belly and moving away from the fight and to the gate. It opened and two men rushed in, dragging the man away.

Ira pointed at the gate then the man Rota had disabled. Two more men ran across the cage and pulled the man out. Leaving two still standing.

"You know they still expect a kill," one of the remaining men said, pointing his knife at Rota. "Or three."

Rota jutted her chin and bent her knees. "Let's see what you've got then."

The last attackers closed in, knives flashing, flesh splitting open, their blood decorating shirt and skin and floor. Ira punched one man so hard, Bryn heard the jaw break. The man went down; Ira dragged him to the gate and dropped him.

Bryn stepped in front of Rota, facing the last man. "He's mine."

She switched the knife to her left hand and fisted her right. She slashed and punched, pushing the man back until he was against the cage wire. With an upper cut, she dazed him; with a pair of slashes, she cut his forearms.

His knife clattered to the floor. Bryn raised her hands to the crowd, expecting a roar of approval, but she was met with mutters.

"Get him out of here!"

The man was led out. The gate closed.

Bryn joined Rota and Ira. "It's done then. Let's get out of here."

174

Rota stared at the gate, horror growing on her battered face. "I'm afraid not."

Bryn turned to see what Rota was looking at and saw Mr. C and his sons, their wide grins nearly maniacal.

"This was just an appetizer," Rota said.

Ira grimaced just as the loudspeaker crackled.

"Ladies and gentlemen. It may look like the fight is over, but that spectacle was just the warmup. Courtesy of our new partner, Mr. Caldwell, and the dramatic entrance of our surprise guests, we will now begin the final event of the night, a three-way fight to the death. Only one will walk out alive."

The subdued crowd came back to life. The betting on the match soared to a rabid pace.

"What?" Bryn asked, stunned.

"You didn't think they'd allow the fight to end with the three of us still standing, did you?" Rota asked.

Ira wrapped an arm around Bryn's shoulders.

"I'll take a fall," he said quietly.

Bryn jerked out from under him. "No! None of us is dying, not here, not like this. We'll fight our way out and I'll kill Mr. C and his sons while we're at it. They'll never bother you again," she said, turning to Rota. "Either of you."

Rota shook her head. "I'll take a fall too."

"No! The horses need you," Bryn insisted.

Ira took Bryn's right wrist and lifted it, pressing the tip of the knife in her hand against his chest, over his heart. "Like you said, Rota can't be allowed to kill."

"Then we climb the fence and get out of here," Bryn said.

As if she'd been overheard, an alarm blared. The crowd surged away from the fence. A loud pop sounded, followed by a low humming.

"What was that?" Bryn asked.

"The fencing is electrified. We climb, we fry," Rota said.

Bryn struggled against Ira's grip, but he was too strong. "So, we kill each other?"

"It's the only way to get out of this cage and protect Rota." He leaned down and whispered in her ear. "Do you trust me?"

Bryn grunted as she fought him. "I don't even know you."

Ira wrapped an arm around her waist and pulled her against him. "Then trust that I don't want to die any more than you do."

"I don't see another option here," Bryn said, looking up at the giant man softly grinning at her.

"Rota, one thing," Ira said, not taking his eyes off Bryn. "Do *not* let them separate us. Understand?"

"No," Rota and Bryn said simultaneously.

"No matter—just do it. If you can keep Bryn pressed against me, chest to chest like this, even better."

"What are you doing?" Bryn whispered.

"Making this right."

He lowered his head and kissed her softly. Bryn inhaled sharply at the intimacy.

"Sorry," he said, lifting his head. "I've wanted to do that since I first saw you."

"I already kissed you," she said, dazed by the fire the gentle kiss had elicited.

"Not like this," he said, lowering his head again.

The fire racing through her exploded into a conflagration. She pressed against him as he plundered her mouth, beckoning for her to open to him, she unable to deny him anything. Not if it meant he continued tearing her apart and putting her back together.

He finally raised his head but held her tight as she sagged.

"You kiss me like that, and now we kill each other?" she asked, incredulous.

"Uh-huh."

"Well, damn."

A small chorus of boos ran through the spectators.

"Ready?" Ira asked, lifting his knife and placing the tip over her heart.

"Odin help me," she said, closing her eyes.

"Take my blade hand and I'll take yours."

She nodded, her eyes still shut. She wrapped her hand around his and leaned in slightly, just enough for the blade to pierce her skin.

He held her hand. "On three."

Bryn nodded again, too shocked to speak. She didn't have any words; the trembling of her body said everything. Pain was never fun, but she'd lived through plenty of it. That didn't scare her. Trusting this man, one she barely knew, and she only now recognized she wanted to learn more about, was a revelation. Considering how far he was asking her to trust him and that she was going to, it was a bombshell that scared the crap out of her.

"One."

Her breath hitched; her heart thudded against her chest as if it knew it was about to be assaulted.

"Two."

She stared into Ira's eyes, saw the peace and calm, and tried to relax.

"Ready?" he asked.

Her heart leaped into her throat. Nodding a third time seemed childish, but that was all she had the strength to do.

"Three."

They pushed the knives into each other.

Bryn gasped, the pain stealing what little breath she had. She fell but Ira held her tight against him, his face white, the creases in his face the proof of his agony.

"Odin," Bryn said, darkness growing around her, the cheers of the crowd fading to a buzzing.

Then, nothing.

31

Bryn felt before she saw or heard. Heat bloomed on her chest and over her belly, a circle with many disparate points of warmth inside it like a sigil, but one she didn't recognize from the unusual touch.

She opened her eyes and saw Ashton's bed across the room. *Is this Valkyrie heaven? A life in a room shared with a horse?*

She couldn't imagine a better place to be.

Then a deep *lub-dub* vibrated under her ear.

She turned her head and looked at Ira's sleeping face. Handsome, peaceful, strong, not just in the sharp angles and planes, but in the surety the man seemed to possess.

She shifted and the covers slipped off her, exposing her position.

Buck naked, on top of Ira's huge chest, with something monstrous between her legs.

"Holy shit!"

She rolled off him and the bed, hitting the rug-covered floor hard. Scrambling up, she covered her body with her hands and looked for some clothes.

"I was having such a wonderful dream too," Ira said, his eyes still closed, his huge erection poised to seek and destroy the nearest vagina.

"Not gonna be mine," Bryn said under her breath, diving for the robe draped over the chair at the desk.

She wrapped the soft chenille around her and secured the robe closed with the belt.

Ira opened his eyes, saw her face, and laughed even as one of his magnificent blushes bloomed. He reached down and pulled the top sheet over him, the tent in the sheet doing nothing to hide his interest in her.

"Sorry about that. It's been a while."

She pointed in the direction of his mid-belly. "Tell it to stand down. Not happening."

Ira rolled onto his side and propped his head on one hand. "How do you feel?"

"Like I died and came back to life. How did that happen, exactly?"

"My special gift, the one every Ira gets when he reaches adulthood."

He motioned for her to come to the side of the bed.

She eyed him, suspicious of his intent. "What?"

"I want to show you something."

She crossed her arms over her chest. "I think you've shown me enough."

Another blush. "Not that. Come, don't be chicken."

She grunted. *As if.*

Bryn walked closer, ready to leave the room if he tried anything hinky.

He pushed the sheet down to his lower belly, baring his impressive eight-pack. He pressed her fingertips to a spot just below his sternum. "Touch the scar."

Her curiosity won the day. She sat on the side of the bed and touched the white, puckered skin.

"Push harder."

Pushing deeper, her fingers found a rigid mass under his skin. "What's this?"

"It's what makes me special. You know about the first Ira who was a priest to King David? Well, in the time of Solomon, that same Ira was well trusted by the king. So well trusted that when Solomon hid his great treasure, he gave Ira this gift and commanded that every Ira protect it until the gift is needed."

Bryn worked her fingers around the edges. "What is it?"

"It's the Seal of Solomon, his great ring. It's imbedded in my skin, and the reason we both lived."

She pulled her hand back and stood. "You knew we would survive?"

"I knew I would survive; I took a gamble that if you remained with me, in contact with me, that the ring would save you too."

She backed up a step even as she itched to slap him silly. "You gambled? With my life?"

He shrugged, oblivious to the danger he was in.

She bit the inside of her cheek to keep her brain from stroking out from the restraint she was having to exert.

"I've saved birds and other animals this way."

"But not people?" she asked, her voice squeaking.

His eyes widened as if he finally realized just how upset she was.

"I had no reason to think it wouldn't work. It did work," he said, gesturing toward her with one hand.

"Oh!" she bellowed.

Grabbing a pillow, she beat him about the head and chest.

"Whoa, hey, stop that," he said, his hands up to defend himself.

She kept at him until the pillowcase seam broke, as well as the pillow, and feathers flew around them. Ira reached up and grabbed her around the waist, easily pulling her on top of him. Bryn pummeled him with her fists, her anger winding down, leaving her with the girliest of tears.

She sobbed and collapsed against his chest. "Look at what you did! I never cry!"

He stroked her hair. "There, there now. You've been through a lot in a short time. Let it out."

She pressed her face into him and let go of her fears and frustrations, of the terror of the fight in the ring and the moment she felt her heart stop. She heaved and sobbed, coming undone, something she hadn't done since she was a child.

Ira simply held her and crooned.

She slowed and the sniffling started. "I need a tissue or twenty."

Ira lifted the corner of the sheet. "There's plenty of acreage here."

Bryn lifted her head, took the proffered corner, and laughed. "Rota would have my hide." She pushed off him and sat on the edge of the bed, reaching for the tissue box on the nightstand. "Why are you being so nice to me?"

He cocked his head. "I think I have a crush on you."

"What? You like my abrasive attitude, my smart mouth, and my scars?"

"Yep, I'm kind of a sucker for difficult women."

"You must be kidding."

One of his eyebrows rose and he placed his palm against her forehead as if checking for a fever. "You met my mother?"

Bryn snorted, then blew her nose…again. "You have a point." She sagged and looked at Ashton's empty bed. "I wonder what's happened since we, you know, died."

"Rota was declared the winner and we were dragged out together. Rota made good on her word, threatened to mess up anyone who tried to separate us. Then the funniest thing: Mr. Aries showed up at the fight and took over. He had his men bring us here at Rota's insistence. Then he found the cameras I had planted around the mall and over the cage. Aries also hacked into Mr. C's computer with the passwords I left for him and let the organizers of the fight know that Mr. C had planned to shake them down so he could take over their fights."

"How do you know all this?"

"I've been awake for a while now. Rota's been filling me in."

"And I've been draped over you this whole time?"

He smiled. "Yeah, and I need to pee like a racehorse."

"Why didn't you…you know?"

He pushed Bryn's hair away from her face, his eyes soft as he brushed a thumb along her scar. "I couldn't risk your life."

"Oh."

Ira dropped his hand and cleared his throat. "So, Mr. C and his sons are on the run from some very pissed-off, very well-connected, very rich people."

Bryn grinned at that. "What about the fights?"

Ira laughed. "Funny how the same videos were sent anonymously to the F.B.I. in Denver. They'll be very interested in the fights and the people betting on them. Rota's talking about taking control of Mr. C's fight club and turning it into a legal one. There's a lot of good men out there that could use a hand up. She's going to give it to them if they let her."

"And you?"

"I'm going to help her there, and here at the ranch, if she agrees. Seems I've developed a real fondness for ranch work."

Bryn rose at that and grabbed her clothes, discomfited by the idea of the two of them…together. She needed to speak with Rota, now.

Walking to the sliding door, she rested her hand on it. "Ira?"

"Yes?"

"Thank you for saving my life," she said softly, without looking at him.

"You're welcome, Valkyrie."

* * *

Bryn dressed quickly and trotted to the great room. Helena and her brothers sat at the bar, handing out chunks of watermelon to Ashton, while he dribbled and drooled on the floor.

"Making quite the mess, I see," Bryn said.

"Bryn!" Helena yelled, jumping up from her stool. She ran to Bryn and threw her arms around her, hugging her tight. "We were getting worried that you'd never wake up."

"How long have I been out?" Bryn asked, wondering why she hadn't thought to ask Ira.

"Three days. You've been in the bed with Ira for three whole days," the girl said, her eyes dreamy. "Naked."

Bryn planted her fists on her hips. "He's too old for you."

"Maybe, but he's still dreamy."

"Odin help me. Go back to feeding Drooly Pants over there and leave the boys to the grown-ups."

"I agree wholeheartedly," a man said from the hallway leading to the barn.

He walked into the room.

"Daddy!" Helena and her brothers said at the same time.

The three jumped down and ran to the tall, blond, blue-eyed, Nordic god filling the room.

Aries was even more stunning in person than he had been on Facetime.

He nailed Bryn with a look. "You must be Bryn."

She nodded once. "I owe you thanks."

"Not even remotely. I'm here to thank you for helping save my children, my home. Taking down Caldwell was the icing on that delight."

Helena leaned back and looked up. "Where's mom?"

"At home, assessing the damage done by the intruders."

"Mr. C's sons and friends," Bryn said.

Aries touched Helena's cheek. "And figuring out who accessed the basement storage area."

Helena opened her mouth then closed it again.

Smart girl.

Bryn decided to help the girl out. "Is Rota around?"

"She's in the arena," Aries said, extricating himself from the trio. "Children of my loins, go outside and get some sunshine, you pale heathens."

Helena ran to the sliding door and opened it for her brothers, who charged outside, roaring at the top of their lungs like Berserkers. Helena rolled her eyes as she closed the door.

Aries watched his children. "I know you and Helena saw more than you should have."

"Rota."

"She doesn't keep secrets from me, nor I her. I also noted a missing book."

Bryn gritted her teeth for a second to rein in her temper. "The book will be returned to you, after you explain why you have a frozen Black Zodiac."

"You do realize I don't answer to you."

"True, but I would imagine the Zodiac Assassins would be interested to know about the time bomb you have stored under your house."

"If you tell them, you better make it clear that all of the families have their Black Zodiac 'under their house.'"

"All twelve still exist? How could you?"

"Self-preservation. I'll be expecting that book. No later than tomorrow."

Bryn smiled. "I'll be sure to send it with Helena. You'll have it when she returns home."

"No, no, give it to Nan. Not Helena."

He blanched and shuddered slightly.

Most would have missed it, but Bryn was looking for it. "Alright, Nan then."

He nodded then walked outside to join his kids, his face paler than it had been when he first entered the room.

32

Bryn chuckled. So, Aries did have a weakness and Helena was it. Maybe his wife too. Pulling her hair into a ponytail, she left the great room and headed for the arena. She leaned against the corner of a stall and watched Rota run her hands over a young foal, sensitizing the baby to being touched.

The mare stood close by munching on a pile of hay, not a care in the world, a testimony to the trust Rota had earned.

Bryn stayed in place until Rota finished and walked away from the pair, leaving the foal to explore, the baby a little too young to be out in the pasture with the other horses.

Rota changed direction when she saw Bryn. "You must be feeling better."

"I am, and thankful to be alive."

"You should be. I had no idea Ira had such power."

Not the only power the man has.

Bryn mentally shook her head. "The horses back?"

"As soon as you and Ira were situated, I got the kids and sent the horses home." Rota stuffed a couple pats of hay into a rack in the stall next to them. She picked up a couple more and headed for the next stall. "Want to help me hay the rest?"

Bryn settled into the simple work, reveling in the sweet smell of the hay, the warm scent of horse, even the not entirely unpleasant odor of manure. They worked in tandem until all the horses in the arena and in the barn had hay.

She loved it here and could see herself staying, but the call of the horde pulled at her. Her people needed her to stick to the mission at hand. It wouldn't do to dwell on what could be, not when reality was so dire.

"Rota, I need to go back to the horde, even if you won't. It's where I belong. And I'm taking at least one flying horse with me as proof, so I can persuade them to turn back to Odin."

Rota sighed and looked away.

Bryn's heart sank.

"I appreciate what you and Ira did for me more than I know how to say, but that doesn't change my mind. I see your potential, I see that you're close to retaking the oath to Odin, I see that you've already changed since we first met, but the horde's problem is still the same. Horses will never fly for them if they continue to turn their backs on Odin. You can leave when you want, but you won't be taking any of my horses with you, not when your inevitable failure to convince the horde would doom them just as it has the rest of the Valkyrie mounts."

Rota scuffed the ground with the toe of her boot, her head down studying the dust she was kicking up. "Or you could stay here and help me."

Bryn sucked in a breath, aware of the honor Rota was giving her. "I can't stay."

Rota raised her head, her expression flat, and stared at Bryn for several seconds. "Then there's nothing more to say."

She left Bryn behind and walked to the house.

Ashton trotted past Rota and made his way to Bryn.

She opened her arms, and he pressed his head against her chest. "Hell, horse, I'm going to miss you."

"You're leaving," Helena said in a small voice.

Bryn kept her head down, refusing to let the girl see her tears.

"The horde," she managed to choke out.

"What do they have that we don't?"

"It's not that simple, Helena. They need me to help them survive."

"Why does it have to be you? Aren't there many of them? We need you here," she said, her voice plaintive.

"You don't need me. You have your family and Rota and the horses."

"But—"

"I'm sorry, kid. I don't have a choice."

Helena's hands clenched into fists. "You always have a choice. Too bad you're about to make the wrong one."

She turned and ran away.

"This really sucks," Bryn said.

Ashton pushed against her then trotted off to a section of grass and started eating.

The weight and heat and scent of the horse was gone; Bryn had never felt so alone. To go back to the horde with nothing was as painful as leaving this place. But there was nothing for it.

The sun streamed through the barn windows, the angle steep. It was late in the day. She left the barn and stood under a tree watching the horses race through the pasture, their manes and tails flowing in the breeze, their necks curved, their galloping joyful. The warm light painted their rippling muscles and glossy coats with fire, their beauty as great as the goddess Freyja.

Called forward, she walked to the fence and clung to it, memorizing the sight for the future when despair gripped her.

Suddenly the chestnut horse Rusty, the one who'd rejected her, broke from the pack and raced to the fence, stopping short of hitting it. He tossed his head, his wings erupting to stand tall over his back, his red feathers filtering the setting sun.

Bryn gripped the fence tighter, struggling not to pant at the sheer beauty of the display.

Rusty dropped his head, then slowly dropped to his knees.

"An invitation," Bryn whispered.

She glanced back at the arena; only Ashton would bear witness. Without thought, she climbed the fence and dropped down to the grass. Running to the waiting gelding, she threw a leg over his back and gripped his mane.

Despite her decision to commit to Odin and try to convince the horde to do the same, she didn't hold great hope that he would allow her to fly, especially after killing without his sanction, but the need to do just that drove her to try.

"Fly for me, boy. Please."

Rusty climbed to his feet, shook his head, then took off at a run, his white wing tips hitting the ground as he flapped hard.

Bryn's heart thudded in her chest.

His muscles bunched under her, then he leaped.

The ground fell away; the wind rushed over Bryn's body. Rusty leveled out and she sat up, throwing her hands into the air.

"Woo hoo!" she screamed, the thrill of flight coursing through her.

Her heart pounded, pulses of electricity racing over her skin. The power—the purpose—filled her until she thought she'd burst from it.

The air vibrated.

She looked back and saw more horses had joined them, flapping hard to catch up, the light from the near setting sun branding them. This was the glory of flying. This was the bond between Valkyrie and horse that she'd desired. This, or rather the absence of this, was why the horde was dying off.

The sky was wide; there was nothing to stop her from heading to her people, Rota be damned.

"All the way then, Rusty," she shouted. "To the Valkyrie."

Rusty turned his head slightly to the left and flapped hard. He'd heard her, he'd understood, and he'd accepted her call.

Bryn closed her eyes and let the joy of her success permeate.

A squeal caught her attention.

She looked down and saw Ashton galloping along the ground, struggling to keep up. His wings had unfolded from his back, but the feathers were fragile—several were missing. One long feather fluttered away as he raced along a road that made a hard left, a long, steep cliff directly in front of him.

Bryn waved at him. "Go back, Ashton. Don't follow us!"

The older horse kept running, lather forming then dropping off him with every step.

"Odin, stop him."

The god did nothing; Ashton grew closer to the drop off and at the rate he was going…

Bryn grabbed Rusty's mane and gripped him tight with her legs. "We have to stop him."

She leaned hard to the left to make him bank. She pushed him to continue the hard turns until he was in front of Ashton, just barely above the road.

Bryn twisted at the waist and threw her left hand up. "Stop!"

Rusty grunted, his hooves touching the ground.

She looked around and her heart sank. The cliff was upon them.

Rusty pushed off and the ground fell away.

Bryn looked back again. "Ashton! No!"

He leaped out into the air, his wings flapping, feathers falling off with each effort.

She leaned to the side to get Rusty to bank again, but the rest of the horses had caught up with them. Rusty screamed as another horse crashed into them, their wings tangling.

The horses fought to free themselves.

Feather and bone beat against Bryn. She threw up her hands to protect her face, at the same time as the other horse's wing hit her in the ribs.

Time slowed as she flew off her mount.

She hung in the air. Then time sped up again and she fell, screaming. There was no surviving this, there was no Ira to bring her back, there was no prayer that Odin could answer; she was going to die.

Bryn panted through the panic until a shadow fell over her.

Ashton hit her legs.

She cartwheeled through the air, grasping for something that wasn't there, but unable to stop the impulse.

He circled back and soared under her, coming in too fast. A few feet away, he beat his wings hard, leaving behind a flurry of feathers, and slowed. He stopped flapping, letting his body free fall.

She grabbed the tip of one wing and pulled her way down it until she could seat herself on his back. "Holy shit, Ashton. That was brilliant!"

He flapped his wings, but the speed of their fall didn't slow. He kept trying, his body growing tenser by the second.

This was why Ashton didn't fly anymore. Why Rota discouraged it. He couldn't fly, especially not with a rider.

The woods and rocky ground rose quickly. There was nothing to do to stop the crash.

Ashton raised his wings and enveloped Bryn, doing nothing to slow his fall, doing everything to protect her at the expense of his life.

"No!"

33

They hit the ground hard.

Ashton groaned once and sagged; his wings fell open, almost bare of feathers, just torn skin and broken bone left.

Bryn rolled off him and collapsed between his four shattered legs. She lay still for a long time, shocked that Ashton was still alive, still breathing.

Nausea gripped her. She crawled away and vomited until her belly was empty but that didn't make her feel any less sick. She made herself look; she could at least acknowledge what Ashton had done for her and stay by his side until he was gone.

She returned to him, going to his head, her heart sinking at the damage the earth had wrought to his large but fragile body.

"Why? Why did you come after me?"

The tears rolled down her face as she sobbed. Her hand shook as she reached out and gently pressed her palm to his jaw. "Please, Ashton, don't leave me."

Even as she said the words, wishing more than anything that he would miraculously stand up and shake it off, she knew his time was near. She pulled the relic from under her shirt and gripped it tight with her free hand. She would give anything to buy him that miracle.

Bryn pulled the leather thong over her head and stared at the piece of Odin's sword. It was her connection to him, her birthright, her chance to become a Valkyrie horsemaster.

She kissed the etched metal. "I give up all of that, Allfather, to give Ashton your gift of life, to give him a second chance. And if you won't do that, at least spare him the pain of his end." She pressed the metal against Ashton's chest, right over his slowing heart. "I pledge myself to you, Odin. From this day forward, I will rededicate myself to the oath the horde has forsaken."

She dropped her head and closed her eyes, seeing the paintings of the Allfather, willing him to hear her. "I will stand in service to the House of Aries. I will lay down my life to ensure their welfare. I will do everything you ask of me…just… please…save this horse."

She repeated the words under her breath, over and over, not stopping until the relic under her hands grew warmer to the touch.

Ashton snorted and tried to lift his head.

Bryn used one hand to soothe him, keeping the relic in place with the other.

Dark had fallen, but the metal shard began to glow.

"Yes, please, Odin, accept my oath," Bryn whispered.

The relic sank into Ashton's chest, disappearing.

Bryn fell back.

The small glow that had dissipated the night grew brighter until she had to throw up a hand to block it. It spread throughout Ashton's body and down his broken legs.

He lifted his head then rolled up. He remained in place for several minutes then tucked his legs under him and stood, shaking as if he'd just woken up from a nap.

"Oh!" Bryn cried out. She scrambled to her feet, running her hands over him. "You're healed. Odin be praised. He brought you back."

She threw her arms around his neck and cried again. *Seriously, this has got to stop.*

The only saving grace was she had no witnesses.

"Well, of course Odin brought him back," Rota said behind her.

Bryn turned her head. The horsemaster stood with her feet spread and her arms crossed over her chest, her tear-soaked face belying the belligerent stance.

Behind her stood Ira, grinning broadly.

"You pledged to fulfill your oath to him," Rota added. "Not that you're going to escape the ass beating I'm going to give you for trying to steal Rusty and almost killing Ashton."

Bryn released him and copied Rota's stance. "I'll happily take the beating, as long as you accept my apology."

They stood there for a moment until Rota cupped one ear with a hand.

Bryn blinked. "Oh, yeah. I am so sorry that I tried to steal Rusty and almost killed Ashton." Her hand drifted to Ashton's back. "More than you'll ever know. I hope you'll forgive me."

"Humph." Rota dropped her arms and went to Ashton, wrapping herself around his head and squeezing. "You gave me a heart attack, my friend. No more flying, okay?"

He snorted then lipped her jeans pockets for a treat.

"You going to give up pestering me about the horde?" Rota asked.

Bryn's heart flopped and she looked out across the horizon. "I'll never stop hoping the horde will turn back to Odin, especially now that I've seen the proof that he's still out there, listening to us. I have to communicate that to them; I must convince them to change. They're my family." The broken, leather thong that had held the relic dropped out of her hand. "But going back isn't an option anymore. They'll never allow me to be a horsemaster without the relic, and now that I've rededicated myself to the oath, they'll never allow me to live among them. At least here I can be a part of what you've started."

"Will that be enough?" Rota asked, releasing Ashton, who'd spotted a patch of grass.

Bryn swallowed hard, her tears too close for comfort. "It will be, with time."

Rota wiped her hands on her jeans. "Well, that's good because I'm about to work you into the ground."

"Oh? The horses aren't that hard."

"I'm not talking about the horses."

Bryn waited, impatiently, but she waited.

"It's the ground we're going to have to break on the new barns and houses."

Remaining still, Bryn waited. Rota started walking to her truck.

"We're going to call the horde tomorrow, tell them what has happened here, what you've learned," she called out over her shoulder. "I'll provide video proof if that will sway them. I will even welcome them here to see for themselves if it will help. They can come here and live, if, and only if, they rededicate themselves to Odin." She opened the driver's side door. "We'll see if any of them choose wisely."

Bryn forced herself not to squeak. Talking with the Valkyrie, inviting them to come to the ranch, was a huge concession on Rota's part and one Bryn wouldn't risk by squealing like a certain teenage girl she knew.

Rota nodded to Ira, who hadn't said a word, just stood there beaming with pleasure. He walked to the truck and got in. Bryn headed for them.

"No ride for you. You have to walk Ashton back home."

"But that'll take hours," Bryn said.

"Consider it your first chore."

The quiet of the night was pierced by a whinny. Rusty landed at a gallop and headed for Bryn, a few of his feathers broken but the rest of him sound. He slowed to a trot and stopped in front of her. He pressed his head into her chest.

She gasped and lifted her hands to him, petting and scratching him until he broke away and took off at a run. He flapped his wings and lifted off the ground, flying after the rest of the horses.

"Oh, by the way. Looks like you have your mount," Rota called out from the truck.

"Mount? I traded the gift of flying for Ashton's life."

"Seems you've earned Odin's favor; even Rusty has accepted you as his Valkyrie. Get home, get some rest. Your workload has just doubled…apprentice horsemaster."

Rota climbed in the truck, started the engine, then turned around and headed for home.

Bryn planted her fists on her hips, frowning at first, before a huge grin broke out. "Home. Horsemaster." She pumped her fist into the air. "Yes!"

She watched the taillights disappear then headed for Ashton, who'd decimated the small amount of vegetation.

She rested a hand on his neck. "How about giving a girl a lift, big guy?"

Ashton wedged his nose between them and pushed her away before ambling after the truck, his head turning from left to right and back again as he looked for more grass.

Several horses passed overhead, racing and wheeling through the night sky, their shadows flitting between the stars. Bryn opened her arms wide, and smiled even wider, as hope filled her. Hope for herself, and for the fate of the horde if she could show them the life they once enjoyed was within their reach.

For now, she wanted to revel in the change in her own life: the horses, Ira, a renewed relationship with Odin.

Rusty did a fly by just over her head, flicking his tail and completing the impertinence by farting.

Bryn burst out laughing. "Just so, you smart ass. Just so."

EPILOGUE

Aries shut Helena's bedroom door, his heart heavy. His daughter was the light of his life and currently the bane of his existence. Every father dreaded the day that their daughter started dating. He'd been more worried about the day she started asking questions. About who they were, their legacy, and why they had a basement full of antiquities.

What he hadn't expected was for Helena to question him about the mancicle she and the Valkyrie had found frozen in the most secret part of the basement. That one had taken all his resourcefulness to dance around, and yet she hadn't been satisfied with his limited answers. She would ask again and demand a more complete accounting, and soon.

His phone vibrated in his pants pocket, the long and insistent signal spiking his heart rate. He pulled it out and stared at the unbelievable message before running down the hall to his bedroom.

He didn't slow until he reached the basement, pausing to run a hand over the twisted metal of the broken door.

"No, no, no."

He ran through the large book and antiques room, relieved that everything seemed untouched. The door to the smaller room was similarly broken and twisted. Dread settled in his gut, threatening to remain there for a very long time.

He grabbed the damaged door with both hands and tugged on it until he could open it enough to slip inside.

The lights flickered; sparks jetted out from broken wires.

He crossed the room and stopped short, his pounding heart skipping its way to a stop. He pulled out his phone again and pressed one number.

"Marissa, lock down the house. Get the kids and Nan and go to the panic room. No, go now!"

He ended the call then pressed another number.

"Rota, it's Aries. You know that thing we've worked so hard to prevent?" He walked to the man-sized box and touched its mangled top. "It's happened."

He stared inside. "The Black Zodiac is gone."

The End

Be sure to look for the next book in the Zodiac Assassins series: *Aries On Fire*

OTHER BOOKS BY ARTEMIS CROW

Zodiac Assassins series

Lyon's Roar Book 1

Leona's Descent Book 2

Libra's Limbo Book 3

Leona's Cage Book 4

Gemini Asunder Book 5

Abella All In Book 6

Cancer's Moon Book 7

ACKNOWLEDGEMENTS

A finished book takes a team. I want to give my thanks to the people who helped me mold this story into the book you've read today:

Thank you to my two alpha readers, Ashley McGowan and Sharon Baum. They both helped me tremendously by putting eyes on the manuscript and pointing out issues with the story.

To Sharon, thank you for your eagle eyes and your continued support of this series and of me as a writer.

To Ashley, you pointed out a serious issue with the opening and I truly appreciate your help. I also thank you for allowing me to use your baby, Ashton, for this book. It's been great fun using a real horse for this intelligent, impertinent, delightful, equine character. More than that, I appreciate the chance to call attention to a topic near and dear to my heart: animal rescue and second chances.

Thank you to Betty Hussey for allowing me to use her horse Rusty as the model for the horse that becomes Bryn's own mount. Rusty is a beautiful American Saddlebred who is reported to have a huge personality. A goofball and real ham who loves his people! Bryn has to work hard to win over Rusty, and I look forward to having him in more books.

Yes! Both Ashton and Rusty will be appearing in future books!

To Jessica Agee, my friend, thank you for suggesting that I add the Monstrum, the twelve Black Zodiacs, to the series! There's nothing more heartwarming to an author than to have readers invested enough to make suggestions, and what a fabulous suggestion it is! I'm going to have great fun writing these wretches!

To my editor, Sara Litchfield of Right Ink On The Wall. Thank you for your talents as an editor. Thank you for making sure my words make sense and sing for the readers. Thank you for being my friend in Mordor!

To Jane Dixon-Smith, thank you for your excellent formatting and lightning-fast turnaround!

Last, but not least, thank you to my beloved husband. You have always believed in me, and that belief gives me wings to fly. Love you always, my darling.

AUTHOR'S NOTE

It all started with the title, *The Zodiac Assassins*.

While studying writing craft, I struggled to decide what I wanted to say and the genre in which to frame it. Most of my childhood was spent moving from one military base to another with friends coming and going out of my life so I turned to books like the *Wizard of Oz* series for entertainment. Getting lost in each new world fed my wild imagination. That, paired with my adult philosophy that "Anything is possible," primed me to be drawn to the worlds of fantasy and the paranormal. That's when the Zodiac Assassins came to me. Creating the InBetween and the many creatures needed to inhabit it was great fun, but I asked myself, what could I do with it? How could I make these unique creatures interesting and relevant to the human experience? I've always been fascinated by the stars, the universe. The notions of infinity and infinite possibility appeal to my soul. But here on earth, humans are also a source of fascination. Who are we? Why do we do what we do? Then, the Hubble telescope started sending us images of astounding beauty that fired up my imagination. At the same time, I was reading books about astrology and the enneagram personality system. BAM! I had my males and a way to make them speak to all of us. Twelve paranormal males ruled by the shadow side of their zodiac signs who need to overcome the needs, beliefs, and fears that have formed who they are, to become maybe not whole men, but at least less damaged. Fear of emotional attachment, fear of losing control, needing independence are just of a few of the issues that will be explored along with the themes of free will versus fate, good versus evil, and my favorite for this series, the brilliant quote from the television series *Leverage:* "Sometimes the bad guys are the only good guys you get." The Zodiac Assassins and the creatures of the InBetween will face a battle within and without against human, paranormal, and supernatural adversaries. I hope that at least one of the journeys the males must make will resonate with you.

Made in the USA
Middletown, DE
10 March 2023

26530323R00116